I0687476

Her
Tie-Dyed Heart

by

Sarita Leone

The Lobster Cove Series

Her Tie-Dyed Heart

Cover Art by *Debbie Taylor*

The Wild Rose Press, Inc.
PO Box 708
Adams Basin, NY 14410-0708
Visit us at www.thewildrosepress.com

Publishing History
First Vintage Rose Edition, 2015
Print ISBN 978-1-5092-0165-5
Digital ISBN 978-1-5092-0166-2

The Lobster Cove Series
Published in the United States of America

He ran a thumb over the scratch, calculating in his mind how much this would set him back if he took it to the paint guy. And, wondering how the hell he was going to pay for it—the week wasn't over, but last week's pay was just about gone. As usual.

He'd have to fix it himself. Again, as usual.

He turned to the car, parked just shy of where he'd skidded to a stop.

No ordinary car. The Plymouth Barracuda two-door convertible—cherry red—was a thing of beauty. A real getting lucky kind of car if ever there was one. He'd heard it roar, just before it kissed him, so it must have the big 426 Hemi under the shaker hood.

The engine tapped, cooling, as he walked closer. Peering into the driver's open window gave him the second shock of the day.

Even before she turned around, he knew she was a knockout. Gold hair fell onto bare shoulders and through the window, he saw the lithe form as she reached into the backseat.

He'd been hit by an angel!

"Hey, are you all right?"

She whirled to face him. Eyes the color of the ocean on a clear day, turquoise with green flecks. Full, pink lips that begged to be kissed. The kind of face every guy with half a heart prayed would find its way to his pillow at night.

"What the hell kind of cowboy crap was that? You almost killed us! Where did you learn to drive—or haven't you yet?"

So the babe had teeth—and was quick to use them.

Dedication

For Sharon Simpson
My mother, my best friend,
my inspiration.
I love you, Mama.

Chapter 1

"Are we there yet?" The whine was long overdue.

A fast glance in the rearview mirror showed the truth behind the words. A red-faced little girl scowled at the Etch-A-Sketch in her hands. Its amusement factor had worn off—probably an hour or so ago.

Annie couldn't find fault with her daughter. She, too, was past the point of enjoying the long drive. That is, if there had ever been a joyful point in the journey. Which, honestly, there hadn't been.

A move of convenience, that's what this was. And, if they were lucky, it would be a short stint. Although the idea of pulling Sienna from school after school didn't appeal. But the logistics of leaving Lobster Cove could wait—at least until after they actually lived in the place for a while.

"Almost." She reached deep into her reserve of Mother Patience and mustered a cheerful grin, catching Sienna's gaze in the mirror.

"How much longer?"

They were on their fourth day of driving.

"Not much."

"How much?"

A seven-year-old could make the Inquisition seem like a barefoot walk across a bed of powder-soft sand, so Annie shrugged. Calculated in her head. Looked at the clock on the dashboard.

1

"About fifteen minutes. Give or take."

"Give or take, give or take—what's that supposed to mean? You know what?"

Ignoring the question would only bring it a second time, so she responded automatically. "What?"

"Maps are a drag."

"Excuse me?"

"Maps—they're a drag." Sienna tossed the toy. It bounced off the vinyl seat back seats as it hit with a dull thud. Scooting forward, placing her folded arms on the back of the front seat and peering over Annie's shoulder, she sighed. "You showed me the map before we left. Florida and Maine didn't look so far apart, did they?"

Annie looked over her shoulder at the tow-headed child. It still amazed her that such an incredible being belonged to her. That is, as much as one human being could "belong to" another. Belong with? Yeah, she got that. But ownership of? A whole other story.

But if she couldn't lay claim to her baby girl, who could?

"Nope, it didn't." She decided to ignore the "drag" part of the conversation. They were both too tired for reprimands—either giving or receiving. Besides, she pretty much agreed. If the stupid map—crumpled now and tossed to the passenger seat—hadn't been filled with so many tiny, squiggly lines, she wouldn't have taken a detour that put two hours on today's already overlong drive.

The kid was right on. Maps were a drag.

"There's a beach. Beaches aren't a drag." Sienna sounded less grumpy. Funny how the thought of sun and sand could chase away a bad mood.

2

Annie grinned. Yeah, the kid was all hers.

"No, they aren't." The road twisted along the coast, giving them ocean views around corners, then hiding the sight behind big old houses for long stretches. She'd pointed the water out when it first appeared, but Sienna acted disinterested, so she hadn't mentioned it again. Evidently it hadn't gone unnoticed from the back seat.

"Can we go to the beach?"

"You know it, kiddo."

"Today?"

"It depends." Annie hated the all-purpose, noncommittal answer, but the truth was, she didn't know how the day would play out.

"I hate when you say that…"

"Me, too."

She hated a lot of things lately, but hating them didn't make them go away. "Listen, look for Lobster Cove. We should be almost there."

If anyone had told her she would be living in a place named for a crustacean, she would have laughed first, then denied it could ever happen. But, damn if denials and laughter weren't sometimes worthless.

"There!" Sienna's arm shot forward, finger pointing toward the huge white sign visible as they negotiated a final bend in the road.

"Welcome to Lobster Cove. If You Lived Here, You'd Be Home Now." Annie read the sign, slowing to give Sienna time to follow along.

"Will we be living here long?"

Annie kept from answering by reaching into her handbag. Open on the seat beside her, it overflowed with random bits of junk jammed in during the trip. Now, when she needed the directions to the house, she grabbed a tampon. Then, a crayon. And, the receipt from the seen-better-days motel they'd stayed in the night before.

"Will we?" The kid drew out the "e" in one long, annoying drone.

Annie suppressed a shudder, wished she had a Budweiser in her bag and took her gaze from the road for an instant. A scrap of yellow legal pad paper caught her attention, and she reached for it, pushing aside a half-dozen lollipop wrappers.

"*Mom*!"

She looked up just as the front right bumper bounced off a motorcycle.

The shirtless, helmetless hunk riding it caught her gaze—his eyes wide and clearly startled—but the connection was oh, so brief. She swerved. He skidded. And, thankfully, Sienna chose that moment to sit back and keep quiet.

****

Steve Tate heard the car before it rounded the curve.

It took all of his racing skill to avoid being creamed by the chick who clearly wasn't paying attention to the road. As it was, she kissed his rear fender before he spat gravel in all directions and slid to a screeching halt on the shoulder.

He kicked the stand into place, angled the front wheel, and sat for a moment. Damn, but that was close. One second—two, tops—later and she would have hit him dead on.

He didn't get pissed off easily. Generally, he had a level head and open mind. A live and let live kind of guy—no worries, no harm, no foul.

But he plowed his hand hard through his hair. Swore. Finally, he got off the bike.

"Oh, shit." He ran a thumb over the scratch, calculating in his mind how much this would set him back if he took it to the paint guy. And, wondering how the hell he was going to pay for it—the week wasn't over, but last week's pay was just about gone. As usual.

He'd have to fix it himself. Again, as usual.

He turned to the car, parked just shy of where he'd skidded to a stop.

No ordinary car. The Plymouth Barracuda two-door convertible—cherry red—was a thing of beauty. A real getting lucky kind of car if ever there was one. He'd heard it roar, just before it kissed him, so it must have the big 426 Hemi under the shaker hood.

The engine tapped, cooling, as he walked closer. Peering into the driver's open window gave him the second shock of the day.

Even before she turned around, he knew she was a knockout. Gold hair fell onto bare shoulders and through the window, he saw the lithe form as she reached into the backseat.

He'd been hit by an angel!

"Hey, are you all right?"

She whirled to face him. Eyes the color of the ocean on a clear day, turquoise with green flecks. Full, pink lips that begged to be kissed. The kind of face every guy with half a heart prayed would find its way to his pillow at night.

"What the hell kind of cowboy crap was that? You almost killed us! Where did you learn to drive—or haven't you yet?"

So the babe had teeth—and was quick to use them.

Steve held a hand up between them, hoping to slow her down. For the first time, he saw the little girl in the back. She looked fine—smiling through the window as if this minute was the most exciting one of her day. He wiggled his fingers at her.

"I like your motorcycle," the kid called out. "Can you give me a ride?"

"He most certainly cannot," the woman snapped. She pushed open the door, so he took two big steps backward. Having his testes crushed by the chrome door handle wasn't something he was going to let happen. "Wait here—I'll be right back."

She got out, leaving the door slightly open behind her as she walked around him—glaring like a firecracker—toward the front fender. She was even better looking out of the car than in it. Tight denim cut offs, a halter top that showed a flawless expanse of tanned skin, and pink toenails peeking out of a pair of stiletto Candies made just looking at her a treat.

He'd already seen the scratch.

"No…"

The shuddering sigh wasn't what he expected. Her shoulders drooped, and her chin dipped. He thought she would screech when she saw the damage; instead she looked like a deflated balloon. A beautiful balloon—but one leaking air pretty damn quick.

Steve covered the few steps between them.

"It's not that bad." True, she'd hit him, but he wasn't the one with a single tear sliding down his cheek.

The child had slipped out of the open car. She was a miniature version of the woman, minus the sexy clothes. She placed a hand on the fender, running it

slowly over the damage. Then, she looked up.
"Oh, Mama, we wrecked Daddy's car."

Chapter 2

"Fiddlesticks!"

Clarisse Montgomery wasn't above swearing but believed in saving the good ones for when the situation really called for it. Being eaten alive by her own rose bushes was a nuisance but hardly warranted swearing like a sailor.

George was long gone but the love of her life had been an officer on the USS Druid, serving near the Strait of Gibraltar, among other places, during the First World War. He'd been a gentle, kind man—but he'd enlightened her on sailor lingo.

She slapped aside a thorny branch with her left hand while she cut it low with her right.

"There you go—never let the right hand know what the left is doing. Or…is it don't let the left know what the right is doing…" She straightened, put both hands on the small of her back, and winced. Jeepers, but getting old was for the birds.

A glance at the birdfeeder just beyond the rose hedge reminded her that the birds weren't going to eat if she didn't whip up some fresh food for them. It was a time-consuming endeavor, but really, what else did she have to do with her time? What little time she had left to her, anyhow.

"Tipsy, don't eat bees!"

The big marmalade cat's paw stopped mid-air—

mid-swat to be exact—while she turned and cast an innocent look at her owner. The fat bumblebee lazed on a dandelion head, its focus on food gathering—oblivious to the fact it was nearly a midday snack for the feline.

Her hearing wasn't what it once was—who was she kidding? Nothing on her seventy-three-year-old body was as it once was—but the rumble of the big engine caught her attention. Shading her eyes with one hand, she watched the automobile drive up the street. It pulled into her driveway.

"Time to meet our guests." She motioned for the cat, who stood, stretched and followed Clarisse across the grass.

Tragic, that's what it was. Brian leaving behind a family like this, so young and beautiful, and with so much hope for the future. It tore at her heart, seeing the young woman help the small child from the backseat. Her grandson's death wasn't an isolated affair, the way it was portrayed on the news. Oh, no…the ripple effect from one dead soldier just went on and on…and this time, for now at least, the ripple stopped at her doorstep.

Annie looked younger than she remembered. Younger, but older, as well. The reality of life showed in the eyes.

"I'm glad you're here, child. So very glad." Clarisse held her arms wide, praying Brian's widow would welcome a hug. Even without her husband, this sorry duo were family. And family, they had come home.

This was, she knew, the only home available at present. If they had anywhere else to go, they wouldn't be in her driveway.

Annie walked straight into her embrace, and the child followed. When the little girl wrapped her arms around her leg, she reached a hand down to pat the silky mop of hair. It was the same shade Brian's had been, and touching it now brought a twinge to her heart.

"Thank you for having us." Annie's voice muffled against her shoulder. Clarisse felt the tremble in her words, then the shaking shoulders.

The poor girl cried, quietly. So quietly that the little girl never caught on.

Clarisse kissed a wet cheek when Annie pulled away and turned to wipe her face on the back of one hand. A shaky smile, and a deep breath.

It was a tenuous greeting but one Clarisse could accept. Turning her attention on the child, she said, "You must be Sienna. Welcome to Lobster Cove."

A bright grin, so sweet and pure she felt the sun dimmed.

"You're my daddy's grandma, right?"

"That's right. Your daddy was my grandson—my favorite grandson, to be exact."

Sienna bent, swept a palm across Tipsy's back. Then she looked up, her gaze openly curious.

"I like your cat. Mama says we can't have a cat until we get someplace to live."

"Tipsy—her name is Tipsy. And as long as you're living here with us, why don't you let her be your cat. I don't mind sharing, and I'm sure old Tipsy won't mind being shared."

"Really? You'd do that, share your cat?"

Clarisse pretended to ponder. It had been a long time since she'd shared anything with anyone, but this felt right.

"Really. But on two conditions: Tipsy is not to be dressed up in any outlandish clothes. She wouldn't take well to being embarrassed, and I won't do that to her. And secondly, I'd like it if you call me Clarisse. No 'Granny' or 'Grandmother'—nothing fussy or old-sounding. Clarisse is my name, so let's use it."

Sienna looked to her mother for guidance. It was apparent the second request required approval.

Annie nodded.

"Neato. Mom, I knew I had a gran—ah, Clarisse, but who knew I'd get a cat, too? Maybe this place won't stink as bad as we think it will."

"Sienna!"

Annie turned pale at the outburst and would have admonished the child, but Clarisse raised a hand to stop her.

Shaking her head, she gave a snort of amusement. Out of the mouths of babes, indeed.

Catching Annie's embarrassed gaze, she said, "She surely is Brian's baby, isn't she? That hair, those pretty eyes...and that honesty. I like it. There're too many dishonest people in the world. It's about time someone told it like it is."

She looked from child to mother. An unexpected twist to her otherwise-dull life, having these two here in Lobster Cove. They brought a burst of interest to the place, like a shooting star brightened the night sky. However long they stayed, she was going to enjoy the view. Judging by the way Sienna hugged Tipsy's neck, they were in for a display of epic proportions.

****

"Mama, I think I'm gonna like it here."

The night was young, but the day had been long. After a fast dinner of spaghetti and garlic bread, Annie dragged their bags in and unpacked. There wasn't much, so it didn't take long.

Clarisse suggested they share the big corner room on the second floor. Two beds covered in crisp madras bedding, white window shutters instead of curtains, a sitting area and filled bookcase made the space inviting. A bowl of roses scented the air. An ocean view completed the scene. The house sat a few blocks from the beach, but the house had been built on a raised foundation, so the second floor loomed high, affording an ever-changing scene of waves and endless blue above the rooftops.

"Glad to hear it. I hope you'll be happy here, honey. It's a great place to spend the summer, right?"

She wasn't sure how she was going to manage their futures, but for now they could at least have a summer in a beautiful spot.

"Clarisse is a nice lady." Sienna lay on her back, holding her doll, Maggie, over her head. Maggie danced a raggedy sort of mid-air jiggle that was a nightly ritual. "And Tipsy—Tipsy's cool."

Brian's mother had put the stay-with-Clarisse bug in Annie's ear. The idea that perhaps the elderly woman was having problems taking care of herself, and the house in the Cove had been discussed, but now that they'd arrived, Annie couldn't see why anyone was concerned. Clarisse looked fine and fit. The house and grounds were tidy. A few spots needed repainting on the wraparound porch, and the back garden was a bit overgrown, but hey, anyone could understand that kind of thing.

She wouldn't waste energy wondering why they were here. It was a safe place for Sienna, so for now she would make it work. Whether or not Brian's grandmother needed her help, she acted happy to see them. What else mattered?

A large bathroom came with the room. Too tired to fill the claw foot tub, she and Sienna had opted for fast showers, but the day would come, and soon, when she would fill that tub with hot water and let Calgon take her away.

Annie flipped the light switch off in the bathroom. Her shorty pajamas were soft from washing, a little sheerer than they had been when she'd bought them last summer, so when she passed an unshuttered window the warm sea breeze touched her skin. So soft and fleeting...a kiss from the sea, welcoming them.

She shook her head. Overtired, that's what she was. Imagining being kissed by the sea.

Ridiculous!

She leaned down, kissed Sienna's forehead. Pressed her nose against the littler one.

"Good night, angel baby. Have sweet dreams and remember, I'm just over there if you need me."

Sienna grinned, exhaling a Colgate-minty fresh giggle.

"I know. And you remember, me and Mags are over here if you need us."

A nightly ritual. Just tying the strings that bound them together.

"Love you, Sienna."

"Love you, too, Mama."

She climbed into bed, sliding into the crisp sheets with a sigh. So wonderful to feel cared for. So

13

incredible to know she and her baby were safe.

Annie reached out and tugged the chain on the bedside lamp.

Even with the light out, the room glowed. The full moon shone in, creating shadows in the unfamiliar space. Unfamiliar, but not threatening. It was all she could ask for. All she wanted. And, however long it lasted, it was all good.

Chapter 3

Annie slipped into faded denim cut-offs and pulled on a peasant-style white midriff-baring shirt as she kept an eye on her sleeping child. The fact Sienna hadn't awoken with the first rays of sunlight dancing across her cheeks or the chatter of birdsong from the elm outside their window showed how the long drive had taken its toll. It couldn't be helped, but that didn't stop a finger of remorse from stabbing her heart.

She tucked Boo, the stuffed bunny rabbit Brian bought the day they'd learned she was pregnant, down next to Maggie the doll, near her daughter's side. The toy had once been snow white but now, after years of endless cuddling, was more beige than anything else. One ear had been sewn and re-sewn, and still looked held on by a thread and a prayer.

Leaving the bedroom door ajar, she went down the wide oak staircase, trailing a hand along the thick banister. It rose three stories up through the center of the house, solid and impressive. In its glory days, the house must have been a showplace. Generations of living within its walls and the dwindling resources of its current owner had left it shabby—but still beautiful.

Clarisse sat at the kitchen table. A cup of tea, an empty china plate, and an open newspaper lay before her.

"Good morning," Annie said.

It felt strange to walk into the other woman's kitchen, but she would look like a teenager if she hung out in the doorway so she stepped inside.

Annie hadn't thought their hostess would be awake. And dressed, besides. Didn't old folks sleep late, lounge about in pajamas, smoke Lucky Strikes and eat soup all afternoon? This senior certainly didn't fit the image she'd conjured in her mind.

"Good morning." A huge smile. "Thought you might sleep late. Figured you'd be done in by the drive."

"I'd love that, but my body has other ideas. I guess it's the Mommy clock, or something. It came with the baby. Now, I wake early—as soon as the sun's up, practically." She shrugged. "What can you do?"

"Enjoy some quiet time, that's what. Help yourself to tea—or coffee, if you prefer."

Clarisse waved a hand toward the countertop. An open box of Tetley teabags and a china cup identical to the one she used waited. On one of the gas burners on the old white stove, a dented percolator pot. And, a teapot whose spout still trailed a curl of steam.

"Tea works." She made a cup, took it to the table, and sat down. Rather than meet the other woman's gaze, Annie took her time dunking the teabag in the water, then winding its string onto the spoon she'd grabbed from the dish drainer. She put the spoon and bag on the rim of the saucer, then looked up.

Clarisse chose the same moment to lift her gaze from the newspaper. They smiled, an awkward, feeling-each-other-out gesture.

"Like a piece of the paper? It's just the local rag, nothing big and fancy like what you worked for, but we like it. Gives us all the news that's fit to print and the local hubbub, too. Not that any of that needs to be broadcast—mostly around here people have ears to the ground, and the words on the pages are just confirmation."

She took the piece offered. Looked down at the front page. *Lobster Cove Anchor*. Beneath the bold title, a lobster.

It certainly wasn't *The San Francisco Globe* or *Atlanta Journal*. Annie's resume, if she cared to write one, boasted stints with both prestigious news organizations. Her degree in journalism had been put to good use...once upon a time.

Before the war she'd loved her job. Before headlines turned grisly and photos from the field hammered home the point that war wasn't pretty. Never pretty. Less than tolerable given some of the battlefield blood, the dark splotches in photos with horrible captions that sold newspapers, cut too close for comfort.

The war. It had not only robbed her of her husband, her future, and her hopes. It had cost her job, as well. When she couldn't step into the newsroom without crying, Annie knew it was time to quit. So she did.

And now...*Lobster Cove Anchor*.

"Think you might want a job with the paper? I can put in a good word for you with the editor—he used to mow my lawn when he was a kid. I'm sure he'll do what he can for you."

Annie shook her head. She hadn't tied her hair back, so now she brushed it off her neck. The day was already heating up, and it was barely morning.

"No, thanks." She scanned the front page.

Miraculously, there were no war stories. Strange, but encouraging. One reason for coming to Maine was to escape some of the tragedy.

Clarisse tapped one of the two sections still before her with a gnarled fingertip.

"Separate—the war news. The paper decided to put it in its own section, so those who can't—or don't want to—read the day's events don't have to. Sparing sensibilities, they called it."

When it appeared that she might push the war portion of the paper across the table, she sat back in her chair and shook her head. "I don't want to see it."

"I don't blame you." Clarisse folded the sections together and placed them on her lap. "So I take it the *Lobster Cove Anchor* is out?"

"It's out. I can't be around the—well, I just can't." She shuddered.

"No sweat. I'm sure you'll find something to occupy your time."

"I hope so." Two empty, industrial-sized metal colanders were on the far end of the table. Annie pointed. "What are they for?"

Clarisse swirled the dregs of her tea in her cup. Took a sip. "Early blueberries are ready for picking. It's a chore that once started, lasts almost all summer."

"Are there a lot of them?"

"Enough to feed…well, we could feed a whole bunch of people."

Annie knew she'd been about to say, "Enough to feed an army" but had stopped on her account. She appreciated the thoughtfulness, at the same time resenting she put people in the position to wrap their words in cotton lest they hurt the widow.

"What do you do with all those berries?"

Clarisse gave an unladylike snort. "Believe me, they all get eaten. That's after I get purple fingers from making jam, baking pies, and polishing the rest up so they shine at the produce stand. Haven't opened the stand yet this season. Not sure if I'm going to, either."

She'd heard about a stand...A flash of memory. Hot sand. Small blanket. Moonlight. A shared bottle of Bacardi. Then, confidences. All before the lovemaking that pushed all the rest out of their minds...

"Brian told me, ah, one time that the family has a store also. Is that nearby?"

Clarisse's white ponytail gave a confirming bob. "Right in town, by the dock. The store's closed now. A shame, but I had to do it. It's just too much for me to handle alone, so I shut it down last season. But the produce stand out by the end of the driveway—I like to keep that open as much as possible. The tourists love to buy locally grown food. And the ones from New York City? Well, they buy the jams and jellies so fast I can't hardly make enough to satisfy them."

Whatever had Brian's mom and dad been thinking? This woman was in full control of her faculties, and her life. She didn't need anyone to look out for her.

"That's incredible—and you do it all by yourself? Doesn't anyone help you?"

A sad smile. "No one left, dear. I'm the last of the Montgomery line—aside from your sweet girl."

Impetuousness ran in the family. Her mother had eloped with her father. Annie's sister Sarah had run off to become a Barbizon model before the ink on her high school diploma dried. She had married Brian, helter skelter, just a whirlwind love affair before deployment.

And Sienna? That was yet to be seen, but all genetic signs pointed toward her little one being just as spontaneous as her ancestors were.

"You've got me. I'd love to help." It would be something to do, something to free her from her own damn mind, something that had no ties to war or widowhood.

"It's a lot of work."

"Twice as much if you do it alone. Let's cut it in half. So we pick the blueberries first? Then what?"

When Clarisse smiled, her turquoise eyes sparkled.

"First we pick. Then we make jam. And then, if we're still standing, we drop the jars off at the store. Keep a few for the stand by the driveway, but we keep the bulk at the store. Might as well use the space. After all, it's just sitting empty."

Just then, the scuffle of small feet against wooden floorboard. Sienna, wearing a tie-dyed dress Annie had fashioned from an old white t-shirt, appeared in the doorway.

"Morning. Hey—can I play with Tipsy? Where is she, anyway?"

Sienna looked under the table and on their laps. A small scowl.

"She's sleeping. I'm sure she won't mind playing with you later." Annie wished she had a comb to tame the waves hanging around her daughter's shoulders. "Would you like some breakfast?"

Climbing into the empty chair beside Clarisse, the child answered the question with a question. "What are we doing today?"

Annie grabbed a bowl and an unopened box of Cap'n Crunch from the kitchen counter. This didn't seem to be a sweet cereal sort of place so she assumed the box had been bought with Sienna in mind. She poured milk into a glass, then splashed half of it on the cereal.

Setting both down in front of Sienna, she asked, "How about going blueberry picking?"

"Really? Yahoo!" Sienna thrust a huge spoonful of cereal, dripping milk on the placemat, into her mouth.

Annie cringed, wondering what Clarisse would think of an exuberant, and often messy, child in her beautiful old home.

She needn't have worried. Their hostess pulled a paper napkin from a bamboo napkin holder in the center of the table, swiped at the milk puddle, and left it to absorb any further drips.

Smiling, Clarisse tousled Sienna's hair. "Yahoo times two!"

Her daughter giggled, barely catching the milk spray in the palm of one hand. The woman beside her chuckled.

Annie watched, her heart warmed by the exchange. Perhaps perching on the coast in a town forgotten by time was exactly where she and her girlie were supposed to be.

Chapter 4

Annie sat back on her heels. She slid a hand along the back of her neck, wiping moisture off one spot and onto another. Midmorning was upon them, all sultry and bright. Too bright. Her sunglasses were on the dash in the car, and she'd been too lazy to fetch them two hours ago. Now, her face felt pinched into a permanent squint.

Sienna popped what had to be the hundredth blueberry between purple-stained lips.

"They're supposed to go in the colander, you know." She pointed out the obvious just as another berry disappeared. It was hard not to grin when her girl smiled, sending a stream of blue juice dripping off her chin. The t-shirt she wore was a goner. Hopefully the chin would come clean. Her mom gene kicked in. "Really, honey—don't eat too many. You'll get a bellyache."

The blueberry bushes were a long, chest high hedge dripping with heavy berries. Hills Grocery never carried fruit this impressive. Moreover, the grocery stores were probably sprayed with lots of toxins, while these were sun-ripened, rain-watered, and chemical free.

When Napalm could be dropped on human beings without any hint of remorse, fruit for the masses could also easily be tainted. It was comforting to see so many pristine berries.

Besides the blueberry patch, the property boasted several rows of pruned fruit trees. Trellised grapevines. Blackberries. Raspberries. Strawberries. And in a small patch in a corner near a birdbath, something called gooseberries.

How Clarisse dealt with all of it, Annie couldn't fathom. It gave her a headache just looking at the place. So many beds to be mulched. So much fruit to be picked. And forget about the weeding.

On the other hand, it seemed kind of groovy to be able to eat your way around the yard. She'd skip those gooseberries, but the rest of it was tempting.

If she didn't have to weed every square inch, that is.

Clarisse worked tirelessly. She hummed while she picked, and her colander had been emptied a half-dozen times in the big farm sink near the back porch. They hadn't spoken much, just a few casual words as they passed each other on the picking trail.

Sienna chattered as she picked—and ate—so total silences were minimal.

"I think that's about it for this haul." Clarisse stepped back from the last bush in the row. She pulled off her gloves, tossed them onto the top of the pile of berries in the colander near her grass-stained white Keds, and put her hands on her hips. A satisfied smile made her face wrinkles disappear. For a second, she looked almost as childishly joyful as the little girl dancing around her legs.

"Now what? What now—we eat the rest of the berries? Or what?" Sienna hopped from foot to foot. She'd kicked her sandals off, and her pink toenails swished green blades of grass between her toes. "Clarisse? We eat them, right?"

"Good Lord, child—but don't you think you've had your fill of blueberries?" She winked at Annie above the child's head. "I wouldn't be surprised if you don't turn purple while you're sleeping."

Sienna stilled, her eyes wide. "Really? Purple—all over, or just in spots?"

With a shrug, Clarisse bent and picked up the berries. "I don't know. One can never tell with blueberries." She straightened, put the colander on her hip, and led them across the lawn. "But to answer your question: No, we're not going to eat the rest of the berries. These will become jam, and be sold at the produce stand I told you about."

"Okay." Sienna frowned at Annie, furrowing her brows. "Mama, do we know how to make jam?"

"Nope. But Clarisse does, and she's going to teach us."

"I can help, right?"

"Of course. But no more tasting." Annie had no idea how many had actually gone into her daughter's stomach, but the deep stains on her tongue, lips, fingers, and face weren't pretty. "I mean it, Sienna. We're going to make jam—and there's no tasting in jam-making. Understand?"

"Uh huh. Just as long as we can taste the jam when it's done. That's okay, right?"

They placed the colanders in the sink, and Clarisse turned the faucet on. Water splashed over the berries. She turned to Sienna and nodded. "You betcha. If we don't sample the jam, how else are we going to know if it's any good? We've got to taste it."

****

"A lot more work than I thought it would be." Annie lifted the last basket of jelly jars from the boiling water bath. The canning pot, so high and wide, reached nearly to her armpits, but she managed to raise the wire basket—standing on tiptoe—and deposit it on a clean dishtowel on the countertop. She lifted each jar off the rack, using a green-and-yellow woven potholder to keep her fingers from blistering, placing them in a row on another towel. The rows were seven deep and twelve wide. Not a bad tally for a morning's picking.

"Your help made it easier for me. Thanks so much." Clarisse wiped down her old stove, scrubbing the white enamel where it was berry speckled. "It usually takes me twice as long—I guess that's the truth of extra hands making the work go faster, isn't it?"

"Mm hm. No need to thank me. I learned and had fun, too." Annie scrubbed the pots, placed them upside down on the porch just outside the back door. She surveyed the kitchen, her hands on her hips. Then she looked down. Miraculously she'd kept her white top clean—not a speckle of evidence to show she'd been elbow deep in purple all morning.

"Glad to hear it. Now, the jars will go into the wooden crates by the back steps. I'll take most of them down to the store. The rest I'll keep here to display at the produce stand, so they'll be ready to put out for the weekend tourist invasion."

"I'll help." She cast a motherly eye on the child and feline, both sleeping curled on the window seat. "She shouldn't sleep too much longer, anyhow. I don't want her awake all night."

The footsteps on the porch were loud, but she had

been thinking so when she whirled and pushed the screen door wide, Annie ran right into the sturdy male form about to enter.

"What the—" Annie stopped short, nearly body slamming the man. She tilted her head back. Looked up. Scowled. "You."

"Seems we can't stop kissing fenders, doesn't it?"

Chapter 5

She was easy on the eyes. And, the scent of blueberry wafting from her hair every time it swished across those tanned shoulders...well, he'd never gotten excited by fruit before, but this last hair swish had tightened the crotch of his Levis considerably.

"Nice truck." Annie stroked the red leather between them on the bench seat. A fingertip traced a line of decorative stitching, oh, so slowly.

It was a good thing the light chose that second to change. Watching that delicate finger, moving so near, yet so far, from the heat building in him—

Thank God for timing. And traffic lights.

Steve forced himself to concentrate on the road. Not that there was much going on. It was just about dinnertime, and that meant shuttered stores on Main Street, sand-covered beachgoers home and at the dinner table. Hardly any traffic to slow them down. No distractions, either—aside from the berry-scented one beside him.

"Thanks. My father's gift to me when I graduated. He used to take me everywhere when I was a kid. I remember hanging out that window, thinking we were flying. He promised that if I did well in school and brought home a diploma, I'd get the truck."

"So you did?"

He parked. When the key was out of the ignition,

he turned and grinned.

"Yeah. More for the truck than the diploma. I think he suspected but he just handed over the key."

Tightening his fist around the keychain, Steve took a deep breath. The truck had been his father's last gift to him. Three days after graduation, an accident on the lobster boat had left the small town in shock.

"Your father is a smart guy. The incentive worked."

"He was smart. And funny. And hard-working. And…" Eight years, and he still choked up when he talked about his dad. Like an open wound, just waiting to be poked, his missing the only man who'd ever given a damn about him never lessened.

"I'm sorry." The hand moved closer, then cupped his fist. Her touch soothed some of the rawness.

Steve swallowed, thankful his eyes hadn't leaked. Yet.

"Me, too." He hitched a deep breath, then faced her. The compassion and understanding showing plainly in the woman's eyes tugged at his heart. He wasn't the only one battling the grief demon. Time to change gears—and fast. He nodded to the storefront just beyond the vintage bumper. "The store. Want a tour?"

Annie pulled her hand back. "I do."

As they hopped out of the truck, it occurred to him that she'd just uttered the two words that could get a man in the deepest kind of trouble of his life.

****

The interior of the shop was dim, but a good window washing would cure that. Dust flew into the air as they headed to a display counter where two crates were already piled. Steve put his beside them, then reached for hers and placed it on top of his.

"More jam?" Annie asked, pointing to the first crates.

"Maple syrup. This year's batch, or what's left of it."

She peeked over the top of a crate. A couple dozen jars, neatly capped and tied with twine bows. Annie lifted one. Heavy, filled with amber liquid.

"Liquid gold." Steve tapped the jar with a fingertip, and she noticed his hands were no strangers to the outdoors. His thumb sported a callous, and slivers of lighter skin showed between tanned fingers. "Clarisse could make a fortune with this, if she wanted to."

She'd only ever had store-bought imitation maple syrup on her pancakes.

"What do you mean, she could make a fortune?" She slid the jar back into the crate. "How?"

Steve leaned against the counter behind him. Crossed his arms. Looked around at the empty shelves, dusty countertops, dirty windows.

"Back in the day, before her old man checked out, this place was jiving. Really, the place to be. After school, to grab a Coke and candy. High school, cigs, and rolling papers. Moms who didn't want to go all the way to Bar Harbor stopped in for grocery runs. Tourists? Man, they were the real money. What people won't buy when they're on vacation…"

She could envision the place as it had been. Shelves stocked, the sound of children laughing and Coppertone-slathered tourists going for anything made locally—as well as the usual chips, beer, and whatnot.

"What happened? Why close down if it was such a

sure thing?"

He took a deep breath, then let it out slowly. Thinking. She saw he chose his words carefully.

"Like Bob says, the times, they are a-changing. You know, her husband left—pure scandal in a burg this small—and that had to be rough. But she held her head high, didn't let the gossips wear her down. Then, Vietnam. In the beginning, people were scared. What was going to happen to us, if a world away things were exploding? So the tourists stopped coming. For a while. You know how people are, though."

"What do you mean?"

"They have short memories. And the draw of a place like the Cove, so calm and beautiful, reels them back in. They can forget the war, and find some peace—even if it's just for a week or even a weekend. So, they came back. But by that time, the place was…" He swept an arm around to encompass their surroundings. "Like this."

Nothing was as it seemed. Her in-laws let her believe Clarisse old, infirmed, incapacitated—none of which were true. Sure, she was on the other side of middle-aged but certainly not ready to stop living. Sharp, in the mind and memory department, too.

"Why would such a wise woman just pack it in? Clarisse seems full of vigor; it doesn't make sense."

A rueful smile. Sad and small. "She's a one-man band, Annie."

She got that.

"Sure, she's still on the ball but hell, she can't manage everything on her own. We all look out for each other, the place being so small, but she's too proud to accept too much help. No one can put in the time she needs, from what you and your kid did today, to this—manning the place. It's bigger than one person. Especially when that one person is a woman headed toward the final years of her life."

Envy pricked her. Clarisse had had it all once. A home. Husband. Children. Even a business partnership with some meaning, some purpose.

The bones of the shop were still intact. If someone wanted to put the heart back into the place, it might thrive again. All it would take to breathe life into the shuttered business would be a bit of determination. Commitment.

Money.

She had the first two, but the last? Not so much.

Annie sighed. Met his gaze. Shrugged.

Then she borrowed one of Sienna's favorite expressions.

"Getting old must be a drag. Don't you think?"

His laugh was as deep as the navy-blue eyes that rounded in surprise. When he shook his head, the black waves that would have been curls had they been shorter, brushed his shoulders.

"Damn, woman—do you always just tell it like it is?"

"Mm…yeah, I think I do. Just cut to it, no bullshit. Works best, I think."

"Are you sure you're in the right place? You seem kind of citified for the Cove—not that that's bad. I mean, no offense intended."

He had her. Born in Manhattan, schooled at NYU. No denying the city still clung to her. More than she thought, apparently.

"None taken. I guess you're pretty good at cutting

to the heart of things, too. Didn't fool you, did I?"

"Nope. Were you trying to fool me?"

"Do you always ask such hard questions?"

He eyed her, doing the up and down examination that men did without realizing they were doing it. Usually it annoyed her, but the way he did it, looking all tender and inviting, didn't bug her one bit. She waited, knowing that behind the inquisitive stare something brewed.

"Probably," he admitted. "Although I kind of hope the next one isn't as tough as the last."

The suspense was killing her.

"Shoot."

"What do you say we grab some dinner? Head to the beach? Hang for a while?"

She wanted to. Oh, how she wanted to. But…

"Sienna. I shouldn't leave her with Clarisse for too long."

"Why not? I'm sure they're having a blast. Probably baking cookies or painting on the back porch. That's how Clarisse rolls, from one interesting thing to another." He paused, then added, "But hey, if you're worried, why not call? There's a phone booth on the corner."

It sounded good. Too good.

"If they're all right, then yes, I'd like to grab dinner. And see the beach, too. But—" She looked down at her shorts and middy. "I'm not dressed for anyplace much."

Steve cast an openly approving glance her way. He straightened and headed for the door. Over his shoulder, he said, "You're dressed just right for what I've got in mind."

Chapter 6

Gold streaked across the water, orange sun met the horizon. The world looked on fire.

"Is it like this every night?"

Annie took the last bite of her tuna on rye, crumpled the wax paper wrapper, and chewed. The thought ran through her mind that the night was perfect for romance, but she squashed that before it made her do something silly. Like flirt with Steve. Or worse, try to kiss him.

"Not every night, but most. There's just something incredible about the sun touching the water—even if it's just an illusion."

He'd already finished his sandwich, tossed the paper wrapper into the empty deli bag beside him, and had his arms linked loosely around his knees. Now he reached for her waste paper, disposing of it before assuming the reflective position a second time.

She sat Buddha style, her left knee dangerously close to his right thigh.

Drifting on the air from somewhere behind them, KC and the Sunshine Band jived.

I'm your boogie man, do whatever I can... Be it early morning. Late afternoon. Or at midnight...

God, but it had been a long time since she'd danced with a man. Too long.

"Yeah, you're right." Focus on the conversation,

not on her social life—or lack of one. "When I was a kid, I thought the sun slept in the sea. Silly, huh?"

Steve nudged her with his elbow. His warm elbow, which she couldn't help but notice was attached to an arm with a bulging bicep.

"Not silly. Normal kid stuff, I think. Hey, when I was little I was convinced mermaids lived in the cove. Not just one or two, but a whole city underwater. My old man tried to tell me it was impossible, but I'd read the whole Captain Nemo bit and believed life under the sea was probably better than the dry land version."

"Really? You seem so practical. It's hard to imagine you as a little guy believing in mermaids." She grinned, loving the way the tips of his ears colored. A tiny bit pink, that was it—but it was definitely a blush.

"Want to laugh? I tried to find the mermaid city once…shit, I must've been about your kid's age at the time. Walked right out, just past that big tidal pool over there, toward those rocks. Went right in, up past my neck and head."

"That's not funny—your mother must have been out of her mind, watching you do that!" Annie's hand went to her throat. The image of a small child walking into the waves was too much to handle.

"She never saw it. This beach was practically my backyard. We kids used to be here all the time—no parents, just us kids."

Annie couldn't breathe. "Who saved you?" It came out a near whisper.

He shook his head, clearly amused by the memory. "I saved myself. One big swallow of salt water was enough for me. I started to swim back, real fast. And, I never looked for that damn mermaid city again."

They sat in silence for several heartbeats.

"Still think it's out there?" This time she leaned into him, pressing her arm against his. "That mermaid city?"

"Can you keep a secret?" He raised one eyebrow so high it disappeared beneath the wave hanging low on his forehead.

"Try me."

He seemed to weigh his options, like a guy trying to decide between imagination and common sense.

Imagination won out.

"I do," he admitted. Gesturing to the surf at the edge of the beach, he smiled. "Who's to say? So many people think alien abductions are taking place, right? So, hey, who's to say there can't be a whole boat load of mermaids down there?"

Loch Ness monster. Bigfoot. Scooby Doo. Why not mermaids?

"No one. If it's your dream, hold on to it, Steve. Don't be dissuaded by anyone or anything. Dreams are hard to come by, and this one has been with you for so long…I bet you're right. I bet there are mermaids living in the cove…wait till Sienna hears about it—you won't be able to keep from getting the fifty questions about it, I'm afraid."

He stretched out on the sand. Leaned on his elbows. Contemplated the view.

"Cool. I bet that kid of yours asks some damn good questions."

****

Lobster Cove was spit on a windshield. So small everyone knew everything about everyone else in no time at all. So when he'd headed to Clarisse's place to see if she needed anything done, he was aware the hot-headed vixen driving the muscle car was in residence.

Their first meeting had been memorable, in more ways than one. She had been pissed. He'd been ticked off. They'd both snarled a bit.

Steve needn't have wondered if their hard meet was going to be the stage-setter for the rest of their encounters. If he believed in God, he'd be thanking Him. But since he wasn't sure he believed in anything or anyone, he was just grateful the gorgeous newcomer had thawed toward him.

When Annie leaned back in the sand beside him, it took every ounce of self-control not to lean over and kiss her. Damn, but her lips were tempting. And that sweet personality, all wide eyes and sighs—it nailed a chord in him that made his whole body thrum.

Middle of the road, he reminded himself. Stick to light conversation; leave the heavy topics for some other time. Maybe never. That'd be all right with him, too.

"How old is your daughter?"

She took a deep breath, then let it out in a giant whoosh. He glanced over; her grin gentled her features, giving her an almost first-thing-in-the-morning kissable look.

Man, he was going to have to watch his step with this one. A guy knew when he met a heart-melting woman. He just knew, deep in his gut. Right now, his gut was speaking loud and clear.

"Seven. An amazing, wonderful, perfectly fabulous age—and an infuriating, crazy, uncontrollable age, all at once." She giggled, and the sound of the girlishly sweet expression made his gut take note. "I love her more than anything else on this planet, but we have our moments."

"Looks like an angel." He wanted to add, 'like her mother' but didn't.

"When she's sleeping, sure. But I tell you, those curls hide a serious set of kid horns. She can either be so good or...ah, I'll dispense with the PTA meeting correctness and just say it: The kid can be a royal pain in the butt!"

This time, no giggle. Full out laughter. He never expected her to call her kid a pain in the ass; it shocked him so that he burst out laughing. He couldn't help himself—it was funny to hear a mother admit what most of them had to feel at some point in time.

Hell, but he loved an honest woman.

"You didn't just say that."

"Yeah, I did. Really, if a kid's mother can't tell it like it is who can?" Annie swept her hair off her face, turned to him and added, "Don't get me wrong. I adore her. I gave birth to the beautiful being. I would die for her. And I'd kill to protect her. But boy, oh, boy, she can be stubborn sometimes. When she gets an idea in her head—don't even try to dissuade her."

He pressed his luck. "Apple trees make apples."

She arched a brow and met his gaze. No flinching with this woman. No backing down. Just pure steely beauty and courage.

"What's that supposed to mean?"

He shrugged, intentionally making her wait.

She watched. Waited.

"Just a casual observation, that's all. My mother used to say it, that like makes like. Roses make roses. Briars make more briars. Stubborn roses? They have to come from someplace, don't they?" He turned, closing the gap between their bodies slightly.

When she didn't back away, he leaned closer. So close, the tip of his nose brushed her hair. He sniffed.

Speaking with his lips near her temple, he lowered his voice. "But this rose doesn't smell like a rose…it's more like a blueberry rose…"

She inhaled. Held the breath. Turned her head ever-so slightly.

Steve couldn't help himself. He had to taste her lips.

His mouth found hers and it was just as he'd imagined it would be. Soft. Moist. Sweet.

With a moan, he deepened the kiss. For a second her lips didn't part, and a flash of uneasiness shot up his spine. They hardly knew each other—hell, they didn't know each other, and this kiss could get him a fat lip. Or worse. His nuts tightened in anticipation.

No worries.

Her lips parted, and a soft sigh escaped her. So sweet and feminine.

She surprised him again. Tender turned sexy—in a heartbeat. Her tongue slipped into his mouth, and she kissed him the way every man dreams a woman will someday kiss him.

Steve's cock came to attention. Every nerve ending hummed, his whole body alive, fueled by desire and need. It had been so long—too damn long…

He pressed her back against the sand, covered her body with his. He ground himself against her hip, moaning as he sucked her lower lip between his teeth.

"Mm—oh…I—ah…"

Throaty murmurings, they only excited him

further. She wriggled against him, her toned thighs twining with his, moving more excitedly with each kiss.

Then it hit him. Hard.

"Steve—I—ah…"

He opened his eyes. Looked into her face. There was no need for words. Her eyes spoke, loud and clear.

Pushing against the sand with his palms, Steve raised himself and stood. He looked down at her, all disheveled and girl-next-door sexy. Raking a hand through his hair, he turned toward the shoreline.

With an erection practically banging its way out of the zipper of his jeans, he stalked down to the water's edge and did what any man would do in that situation. He began to walk. Fast.

Chapter 7

Sleep had been an elusive bedfellow. Annie's eyes felt like she'd slept in the surf, so gritty and tired it was a chore to focus. The little one had been snoring softly when she'd let herself into their bedroom. Sienna hadn't stirred all night and was still asleep.

She, however, had stared at the ceiling all night long.

Incredible how a kiss could stir so many emotions.

Rising with the sun did have its advantages. Two macramé plant hangers lay in the grass beside her chair. It was not her nature to sit still, except when channeling her creative energy. When it became obvious that she would get no rest at all, Annie grabbed her supplies, made a pot of tea, and took everything outdoors.

The porch railing was an ideal height for working with the long lengths of jute required to knot the planters. A low stool, found in a corner of the potting shed, kept her off the ground. The conditions, conducive to meditative thinking and isolated productivity, suited her mood.

She'd tugged on shorts and tied a halter top on, so as the sun rose higher in the sky her back warmed. Chasing some of the chill from around her heart, her mother would have said. Motherly wisdom stayed with a daughter long after a mother was gone.

So many people missing from her life. So many

empty spots…each person gone, impossible to replace.

Clarisse poked her head out the back door. "I thought I might find you out here." She held a cup of tea in one hand. "Mind if I join you?"

"Not at all. And you don't need to ask—after all, I'm the one invading your yard, remember?"

Clarisse had dressed. Pedal pushers, once navy blue but now faded and patched paired with a black Keep On Truckin' t-shirt. Her feet were stuck in leather scuffs. Not the kind of outfit one would expect from the over-sixty crowd.

As she lowered herself to the top step leading down to the yard, Clarisse shook her head. Her waist-length braided gray hair slid across her shoulder, an emphatic movement to underscore her feelings.

"I could only be invaded by those I don't want in my home. So, my dear, you and Sienna could never, ever invade. I love having you here. Can't you tell?"

A lump rose in Annie's throat. She concentrated on the intricate spiraling knots for a moment. When she'd made a four-inch spiral, she threaded two oversize wooden beads onto the proper strings, knotted them into the pattern, and let that chain drop.

"You're very kind." She picked up the next chain on the planter and began to replicate the spiral. The task went quickly now that she'd decided how big it would be.

"It's not kindness, I assure you. Haven't you heard? Why, I can't believe Brian's parents haven't told you the news."

Uh oh.

"News?"

Clarisse sipped her tea, then went on. "Yes, the

news, my dear. Why, don't you know I'm a feeble-minded, doddering old fool? And a mean, crotchety one at that?"

Annie hadn't been raised by a pack of wolves in the wilderness. She knew when to refrain from commenting. She finished the second spiral, added beads, tied it off and let it drop.

The other woman had no intention of letting the conversation drop as easily as the macramé fell from Annie's fingers.

"Come on, confess. You can't imagine I don't know what they're saying, can you? I may be old—there's no getting around that grim fact of life—but I'm not incapacitated. Surely you can see that, can't you?"

Spreading her arms, pulling the incongruous t-shirt wide, Clarisse waited. Annie was pretty sure she would wait, frozen, until she got a reply.

Diplomacy wasn't a strong point.

"I never thought you would be incapacitated." The final spiral required nearly no attention, her fingers took over and left her mind free, so she met the other woman's penetrating stare. "Really, I didn't. If I had thought that was the case, I wouldn't have brought my daughter to Lobster Cove, would I?"

"I suppose not." Clarisse dropped her pose. She took a swallow of tea, a thoughtful expression on her face. "But you were told I'm feeble, weren't you? Please, tell me the truth."

The beads went on. The strand tied off. Then, it fell into place beside the other two. The planter was nearly complete. Now all she had to do was gather up the three strands, knot them together to form a bowl for a hanging pot, then join them in a decorative knot strong enough to support pot, soil, and plant from a hook on a ceiling.

She picked up her mug of tea. Took a sip. Weighed her words.

No good ever came of lying. She taught that to her daughter. If she wasn't willing to walk the walk, she shouldn't talk the talk.

"No one ever said you're feeble…"

"Aha! I knew it! They did send you to look into what's happening up here."

Annie shook her head in denial. "No, that's not it at all. I admit, I think Brian's parents are concerned about you, but that's because they love you. Not because they think you're feeble. Oh, hell, no! That word? It never even came into the conversation—I give you my word it didn't."

"I believe you. But if I may be so bold, what did come into the conversation?"

No sense stalling.

"Look, it was no big deal, really. I needed a change of environment, a different place with new faces and no sad memories attached to it. And they're of course concerned about you, being all alone in this big place with no one to keep you company. That's natural; they love you, and it's got nothing to do with anyone thinking you're incapable or incapacitated or any other 'in' word you can dream up."

She let that sink in.

"If we're laying it all on the line here, the truth is that this is more about me and Sienna than it is about you. Yes, we all love you and want whatever's best and convenient for you, but that's not the reason I'm here. Maybe I'm too selfish to move across the country to benefit someone I barely know. I'm just not that good a person, Clarisse."

A protest would have come, but Annie held her hand up. If the tactic worked for cops and cars, it should work with elderly relations. It did, but Clarisse waggled her eyebrows in silent disagreement nonetheless.

Annie took a moment, then went right to the heart of it.

"You and me? We each needed something—or someone. Our visiting takes care of both of us. But the one who matters most, to me at least, is Sienna. She's already been robbed—from birth—of one of the most important figures in her life. It's something I can never replace, a hole she's always going to have in her life. I can't help that."

A tear slid down her cheek. She hadn't felt it form, but the wetness on her skin caught her off guard. With a slow fingertip, she brushed it away.

"There may be things I can't give back to my daughter, but there are other things I can make sure she's got in her life." She caught Clarisse's gaze and held it. No room for miscommunication where her kid was concerned. "You're one of the bits of her life I can gift to her. You're her family; the same blood in your veins runs in hers. This place—it's part of her history. I don't want her to miss any of that. So, really, the biggest reason for our being in Lobster Cove isn't you. It's not Brian's mom and dad. It's not me. It's Sienna…and that is the honest truth. It's the only truth I know, the one where my sweet girl gets all she can get out of the life I can give her. That's all I know, Clarisse."

Birdsong filled the air. A salty breeze blew through the trees, rustling the leaves on the poplars beside the greenhouse. Kissed by the sun's rays, cradled in the cocoon of small-town America, it felt as if they were in the most peaceful place on the planet.

Annie squared her shoulders. She picked up all the jute runners, separating them into place in her hands. She began the fun task of creating the pot basket.

Clarisse's teacup was empty, so she placed it on the wooden step beside her. Reaching out, she put a hand on Annie's arm. She stopped working and looked up into the other woman's face.

A smile, pleating the wrinkles around the eyes and mouth. And, tears, slipping slowly down the paper-thin complexion.

"My dear, you don't need to know anything else. Your priorities are so straight, and your heart so full and open—good Lord, that child upstairs couldn't ask for anything more out of life. You're a good mother, Annie. And I'm blessed to have you and Sienna here with me. Thank you."

Clarisse wiped her cheeks with the back of her free hand. A small squeeze, then she took her hand from Annie's arm and set it on her lap.

"Thank you. Not just for your kind words, which I appreciate and oh, boy sometimes need more than anything! And not only because you've opened your home to us—which of course means the world to us. But thank you for letting us be part of your family, for welcoming us with open arms and just pulling us in and making us feel as if this is the exact place we're meant to be. Thank you."

"You're welcome, my dear. Very, very welcome."

They sat in silence for several minutes. Annie looked over once; Clarisse's eyes were closed against the sunshine, her head tipped back and a small smile on her lips.

She finished the plant hanger. Untied it from the porch railing. Picked up the other two, and held them loosely on her knees.

"I should go wake Sienna."

"I'm afraid I tired her out last night. We did play a rousing few hands of Old Maid." Clarisse opened one eye. "And I was, every time, the old maid."

No surprise. Sienna had a way with games, and usually came out on top.

Clarisse sat straight, opening both eyes and picking up her empty cup.

"Before you wake her, I want to let you know about a bit of…well, a bit of unsavory news. I got a phone call just before I came out here. I didn't want to spoil the peacefulness we were sharing, so I didn't say anything but I do want you to know—and without little ears to overhear."

A chill swept through her body.

"What is it?"

"Sometime in the night, probably during the high tide, a body washed up in the cove. A man—a young man, apparently. I'm sure everyone will be talking about it. I just wanted you to hear it from me, without Sienna around."

Annie could hardly catch her breath. She'd left Steve on the beach last night.

What if he went in search of the mermaid city and…?

Oh, no—it couldn't be!

Chapter 8

"When can we go to the beach?"

"Sienna, how many times have you asked that question this morning? Really, do you have any idea?"

Annie's usually wide streak of patience was thin and challenged, having endured the shock of the morning's news and then the never-ending barrage of beach requests. She couldn't tell the kid that there was no way to swim or build sand castles as long as police barricades made the area off-limits. And telling her a body had turned up just where she intended to spread the faded beach quilt—well, that wasn't happening. No better way to give the girl nightmares than inform her dead people were showing up in the sand.

"No. I didn't count." She sat where Clarisse sat earlier. Now, instead of a teacup on the step, a pink plastic egg. The Silly Putty from inside the egg stretched across Sienna's knee.

"Take my word for it, you've asked a lot." Annie twisted the length of jute in her hands more emphatically than was absolutely necessary. "A real lot. And my answer is the same every time, isn't it? We're not going to the beach today. And if you keep bugging me, we won't be going tomorrow, either. So just cool it, okay?"

"But what then, if not the beach? What can we do?"

The macramé planter, her fifth so far—and the day was still young—came together like a dream. The jute was a favorite, some she'd tie-dyed herself last month. The colors were vibrant, and psychedelic. So alive, it made her smile.

This one wasn't going anywhere. She'd find a plant and a pot, and hang it somewhere—as long as Clarisse didn't mind. And if she did mind, the planter would come in handy when they moved on.

"I don't know, honey." She stretched her arms, then her back. Too much time on the little stool. "I'm sure there's lots to do. Places to go and things to explore. We'll ask. Maybe Clarisse has a good idea."

Just then, the screen door slapped open. Clarisse came out, holding bright red ice pops. She handed one to Annie and one to Sienna, then sat beside the girl and licked the one she'd saved for herself.

Almost instantly, after the second or third lick, their hostess's tongue turned cherry red.

Sienna covered her mouth with a hand, giggling as she realized what the ice pops were doing.

"What's so funny, missy?" Clarisse winked at Annie, then opened her mouth wide, letting her scarlet tongue slide along the ice pop in full view. When the little girl pointed, she pulled her eyebrows high. "What?"

"Your tongue!" Her daughter pointed a fast finger.

Clarisse stuck her tongue out all the way, crossed her eyes and looked down. She wiggled her eyebrows, pulled a face and finally gave up.

"I can't see my tongue. My nose seems to be in the way. What's the problem with it?"

Annie watched her sweet girl giggle and lean

against the woman beside her. They'd bonded instantly and were now fast friends. The pairing was working out better than she'd dare hope it might.

Sienna gasped, then licked her ice pop. It was already beginning to melt, trailing a stripe of red down the side of her hand.

"No problem—not if you like a red tongue!" Sienna collapsed into a new wave of giggles.

Annie met Clarisse's gaze. A silent invitation to join the silly parade.

"How's mine?" She stuck it out as far as she could, mimicked the cross-eyed expression Clarisse had pulled off, and was rewarded with a fresh wave of laughter—this time from both parties seated on the back step.

It doesn't get much better than this.

"Mama, yours is red, too. More even than Grammy's!"

Grammy? The two must have come to some kind of arrangement while she was—well, while she was doing whatever she'd been doing with Steve on the beach last night. She was trying not to think about it, what they had been doing. And, how it made her feel. Mostly, how asinine she must look this morning after running off like a virgin at an orgy.

Back to Grammy and company, she reminded herself.

A nod from their hostess. "It is at that, my dear."Clarisse gave her pop a long suck, smiling around the red ice. "What about yours, our little gigglepuss? Let's see that tongue before we declare a winner in the red-tongue contest."

With much giggling, Sienna poked hers out. Of course, they made a huge display, Clarisse covering her

49

eyes, and Annie gasping so hard she began to cough—which brought more giggles.

"That's it, you win! I don't think I've ever seen anything so red." She turned to Clarisse. "Do you agree?"

"Oh, yes. There's no doubt, we have a winner—a blue-ribbon, best-in-show winner, I believe."

"Really? At least I win at something." Sienna concentrated on licking the mess in her hand. The day grew warmer by the minute, and the ice melted quickly. "Even if we can't go to the beach…"

The beach again. Just when she thought the kid had forgotten the blasted beach, it was back in the discussion. Annie bit hard on the ice pop. It was better than uttering a biting word, wasn't it? Not great for her teeth, but good for her daughter's spirit.

She never wanted to be one of those super-strict, spirit-crushing parents. She didn't want to play it so loose and easy her daughter turned into a wild thing, but she definitely wanted the kid to learn to think for herself. Make decisions appropriate for her well-being. Be creative. Crazy. Have fun. Yet, still know the difference between right and wrong.

A hard line, parenting. Especially when she walked it alone. But there had never been a person to share the responsibilities so it wasn't as if she missed that lean-on-me support. Much. She hadn't had it, but she could imagine how incredible it must be to share the biggest joy in life with someone.

"Well, I suppose if you're set on going to the beach, I'll have to save my surprise for another time." Clarisse winked over Sienna's head, then looked dutifully forlorn when the child turned to her.

"We're not going to the beach," Annie interjected. Sticking to her guns on this one.

"Hear that? Mama says we're not going." A long, shuddering, dramatic sigh. She pulled the last of the red ice into her mouth and chewed. Swallowed. Grinned, showing red teeth and gums. "So what's your surprise? If we're not going to the beach, we might as well do something."

"Oh, it's a great surprise." Clarisse finished her treat, bent the Popsicle stick in half, and tightened a fist around it. "Much too good a surprise to be the second runner up, really. I'll just keep it to myself, I think…"

Annie had to hand it to her. The woman had experience shifting a kid's perspective. Sienna had all but forgotten about the sand and surf, and was bouncing up and down on the wooden step.

"Aw, come on, tell me? Pretty please?"

"Nah, that's okay. No biggie." She pretended to examine a cuticle.

"Aw…pretty please—with a cherry on top?" Sienna grinned, looking more like a vampire with red-rimmed mouth and evidence of the ice pop drying on her chin than the sweet little thing she was working so hard to pull off.

"Well…"

Annie couldn't resist. "With two cherries on top? And sprinkles?"

Clarisse capitulated, making a big show of giving in. She put her hands up, mock-surrender style. "Well if you both insist, I'll share my surprise with you."

Then, she sat without speaking. Tension built. Sienna looked ready to burst from her matching plaid shorts and sleeveless crop top.

"Well? Are you going to tell us or not?" The little one leaned close, putting her face nearly on the woman's lap.

Clarisse reached out, stroked one of the ponytails that Annie realized she'd not pulled together. Sienna wasn't proficient enough to put her hair in two tails, her "Grammy" must have done it for her.

It was the first time anyone else had styled her daughter's hair. A small twinge of something—jealousy, maybe?—pinged in her belly. Then, a wave of gratitude washed it away. It was good the two felt comfortable enough to allow the hair session.

"Hold your horses, child. I'm just savoring the moment, keeping this treasure to myself before I set it free. Can you dig it?" Clarisse's use of youthful lingo didn't surprise the child, but Annie had a hard time not grinning broadly. Thankfully, neither of the two paid any attention to her. It was like being a fly on the wall—only outdoors.

"Spill it, already. Please…"

She was glad for the manners practiced without any coaching. Score one for the mom.

"The historical society!" Clarisse rubbed her hands together. Shivered with delight.

Annie prayed Sienna wouldn't be rude; it was written on her face, in her scowl, actually, what she thought of the so-called surprise.

"The what?"

So far, so good. Incredulity was not rudeness, so she kept silent.

"The historical society, of course. Actually, if we want to be proper about it, The Lobster Cove Historical Association. But I just call it the historical society—not such a huge mouthful." The explanation was offered as if she were speaking with an adult, and miraculously the child listened in a similar fashion.

Still, a crease on the young forehead spoke loudly.

"What is it? And is it as good as the beach?"

She shot Annie a questioning glance, who shrugged.

"Better. Believe me, I should know. I work there two afternoons a week. Today is one of my days off—now, really, would I want to go someplace on my day off if it wasn't magical and marvelous? The beach, it's great, don't get me wrong. But the sand and water are always going to be there."

It amazed her, but somehow the kid had perfected the art of the dubious eyebrow raise. It was almost so cute that she—and Clarisse as well, if the look on her face was any indication—almost laughed.

"Probably not. If this hist-hist—"

"Historical," Annie supplied gently.

"Yeah. I guess you wouldn't want to go there so much if the place is crappy." Sienna lifted her hands, held them palms facing the sky, and shrugged. "So it's gotta be pretty cool."

Neither commented on the colorful choice of words.

"It is cool—very cool. Lots of exhibits. Tells the history of Lobster Cove. You can see clothes, books, household things on display, learn how people lived here a long time ago. Very interesting, I think. A surprising place."

They waited, letting it sink in. Annie knew there would be more questions.

"Anything else?" Sienna's probing mind needed

more than old books and dusty bed linens.

"Well…" Clarisse tapped the side of her head with a forefinger. Then she held it up straight, before poking it toward the child. "There's lots of other stuff. An old boat, some anchors. Plaques, but you wouldn't be interested in them. An old fire engine. Some early automobiles. The pirate display, with the gold pieces. An ancient—"

"Pirates? You mean there are pirates here?" Sienna perked up. "Really?"

"Whoa, not so fast. I didn't say there are pirates here now, did I? But there were pirates here at one time. Oh, yes…" She answered the questions before they were asked. Sienna was completely under her spell, and Annie was thoroughly amused. "Lots of pirates. A number of pirate artifacts. Even some pirate 'booty'— which is slang for pirate loot. Oh, yes, we have had pirates here in the Cove. And shipwrecks—lots of them—just beyond the beach."

"You mean when the boat crashes in the water?"

"That's exactly what I mean. It doesn't happen much anymore, but back in the old days it happened a lot. A shoal, a rocky ridge, runs just beyond the cove's opening. In rough weather, ships ran aground on the shoal and went down. Men lost their lives out there. Others were better swimmers, and came ashore."

History had been Annie's favorite subject in college. A passion she and Brian shared. "When was the last wreck?"

"Oh, about a hundred years ago. As I said, occasionally a fishing boat or some silly tourist—drunk and with zero boating skills—rams the shoal but not often. The big wrecks, in the time before cars and planes made travel a snap...now, we had our share. Especially in the cold months, when things up here in Maine can get rough. There were a few really big wrecks...let me see now, some in the sixteenth and seventeenth centuries. We have a few finds from those ships. A ship called the Henrietta...now that's a story in its own right. Interesting, that one. And the Halpern—now, that went down in eighteen-twelve. We've got descendants of survivors of that tragedy still living here."

Sienna hadn't forgotten the pirates. She turned to Annie with a hopeful smile on her face.

"Mama? Can we go to the-the—you know. Where they keep the pirate stuff—can we go?"

Not the time to correct grammar. Not when the beach was forgotten and the adventure was really an educational opportunity in disguise.

She nodded. "I love the idea. But first, we all need to get cleaned up."

Chapter 9

Main Street was quintessential New England. Wide sidewalks beckoning one and all to peek inside quaint little shops, not much more than cubbyholes set side by side, each offering wares which were, mostly, made by locals. Enticing aromas, often from good, hearty, no-nonsense fare, wafting out to pull an unsuspecting passerby in for a bite—or two. Foot traffic that neither bumped against nor rushed by casual strollers.

So went the first walking tour of their new home.

They passed the park. Sienna didn't say a word, but her gaze lingered on the swingset. Another time, they would picnic, beside the white wooden gazebo under the watchful gaze of the nearby monument. A lone sailor, forever looking toward the sea. A testament to the men who had gone out but had never returned home. Sad, yet well-loved, that sailor.

Clarisse so wanted the girls to like the place. Funny, how even Annie had become a girl in her eyes and heart. She knew she carried a woman's burdens, but the grandmotherly instinct inside her was still intact. This woman had been her beloved Brian's wife. And had he lived, he would have seen how wonderful a mother she was to their daughter. Without his presence, there were no others to heap the grandmotherly urges upon; besides, she didn't think Annie would mind being one of the girls.

Truth be told, in her mind she was one of the girls, too.

"I like the colors," Sienna said.

For her age, the child was advanced. Last night, they'd read a book together. Granted, Dr. Seuss wasn't Tolstoy, but the words fell like raindrops from the little girl's tongue. Her verbal ability was stellar, she proved wildly creative when presented with crayons and paper, and now she was astute enough to note details.

It had been a long time since she'd been in close contact with a child, but this one seemed exceptional— even to her untrained, rusty eye.

"You like that? There's a story about it, you know. Way back when, a long, long time ago, people weren't as literate as we are now." She paused, waiting for a question about what felt like it might be a word that required explanation. No question, so she asked, "Do you know what literate means?"

Sienna shook her head, sending her ponytails up and down.

"Really? You do?"

"Yeah. At our last town there was a library. And they had a protest thing outside—you know, where people walk around carrying signs? About the war and stuff?" She waited until Clarisse nodded. "So this day, you know, when I learned that word, we went to the library. No signs when we went in but when we went out, there were signs everywhere. People, too."

She looked to Annie, who just nodded her agreement. The story went on.

"So, me and Mama just crossed through the people. Just kind of walked between them, and nobody bothered us…except one guy. Remember, Mama?"

A look passed between the two.

"He wasn't very nice. He said something mean about people who read too much—what did he say?"

Annie met Clarisse's gaze. Then she looked at Sienna.

A perfect answer coming from a mother. "He was wrong. But he said people who read too much are under The Man's thumb. Remember, the guy was just wrong…"

Sienna looked up. Clarisse knew what was coming next.

"Do you know The Man?"

Shook her head. "Not personally, no. but I do know what it means when someone says that."

It satisfied the little girl.

"Good. So, the guy talking about The Man? Another guy told him to shut up—not very nice—and then someone else called him illiterate. So, when we got home I asked Mama what that means—you know what it means, right?"

Clarisse met the serious stare with a definite nod.

"Good. So that's how I know. There's illiterate and literate—I'm literate. You are, too. And Mama—she's very literate. She's the one who taught me how to be literate, so she's really good at it."

The conversation had taken them nearly to the end of the street. While the child chattered, Annie had browsed the store windows. She lingered at a display of art supplies in Bennigan's. Clarisse made a mental note to inquire about her artistry skills sometime soon.

"Would you like to hear the end of my story, the one about why the buildings along the street are all painted different colors?"

Sienna slapped the side of her face with a small hand. Her cheek must smart, it was hit so hard.

"I forgot—yes, please, tell me!"

Clarisse sat on a bench at the end of the block. The historical society's building was just past the intersection. This spot, however, afforded an ideal view of the row of buildings currently under discussion.

"Well, this is a seafaring town. That means there are a lot of families who rely on the sea for their living. More so in olden days than now, but still, boats go out from our shore every day. They fish for lobster. Crab. Some tuna. Anyhow, way back when, a long time ago, before just about everybody knew how to read, people needed a way to tell things were theirs. Including houses."

Annie and Sienna were an ideal audience. When she stopped, they turned their gazes to the row of buildings they'd just passed.

"Notice anything about those buildings? Besides they're all different colors?"

Annie gave a slight nudge. "Look closely. The colors make them different, but does anything make them look the same?"

Sienna studied the buildings. The point at which realization hit made her eyes gleam. She turned and said, "The same! The buildings are all the same—see, they have that swirly stuff over the doors?"

"Gingerbread," Annie supplied.

"And the windows, they all have…"

"Those are called shutters, dear," Clarisse said. "They can be closed to keep a place protected in bad weather."

"And the roof on that one—and that one—and that

one, too…" She pointed.

Annie's complexion paled. Clarisse saw sadness in her eyes. She answered the unspoken query. "Those are called widows' walks, honey."

The word derailed her. Sienna turned and gave her mother a fast, tight hug. "Oh, Mama…"

"It's all right, baby. I promise. See? I'm not the only widow in the world." Annie pulled a smile onto her face before tilting her daughter's gaze upward. "I'm okay, I promise. And you've got the right idea. The buildings are identical."

Clarisse moved right along. No sense in dawdling over the painful points in life.

"So, you see that the buildings all look the same. Now imagine you're a sailor, home from a long, long journey, and you walk up from the dock toward these buildings. Your family is here, and you can't wait to see them. But—" She pointed to the well-preserved plaques beside each doorway. "You can't read. You're…"

"Illiterate," Sienna supplied, a look of understanding bringing a sparkle to her brown eyes.

"That's right. The only way a sailor might tell one house from another? What do you think?"

"Oh…I get it. They knew by the colors." Sienna looked from storefront to storefront, taking stock of the assorted colors painted on the modest wooden buildings. "Pretty smart."

"The ability to read is not a measure of a person's intelligence, Sienna." She placed a gentle hand on the girl's shoulder and pulled her close. "Please, remember that."

They stood and walked to the corner. A crush of tourists waited, snapping Instamatic shots of each other posing by a huge anchor. It had come from a wreck of little importance, but made an otherwise ordinary corner interesting.

Dodging the crowd, they stepped out into the crosswalk.

"You're going to be pleasantly surprised by all the displays in that humble brick building."

Annie held her daughter's hand while they crossed, with Sienna between them. She looked down when she spoke, meeting the child's gaze.

"What part are you most interested in, honey?"

"The pirates. I want to see the pirates!"

A masculine chuckle caught their attention. They'd reached the other corner—and Steve. He stood, his hands loosely tucked into his pockets, thumbs sticking out. If she'd been a whole lot younger, her hormones would have definitely kicked into overdrive at the sight of the man. But she wasn't, so they didn't—for her.

A glance at the other woman showed Steve's charms were alive and well, and worked just fine on a younger woman.

Pink crept up Annie's neck. Along her cheekbones. Against her bronzed complexion, the hint of color made her even more attractive.

"Hey." Steve gave Sienna a small wave. Then he laid his hand in the air, and she palmed him with her free hand.

"Hey," Sienna said. "We're going to see the pirates. Aren't we, Mama?"

Annie met Steve's gaze. They shared a look—unreadable, but meaningful. Something was up between them, and it wasn't just Steve's palm or Annie's color. There was more…

"Ah, well…"

"Pirates, huh?" Steve winked. He directed his comment to Sienna. "I hear you've got to look real close if you want to see the pirates…"

"Really?"

"Yeah, real close. Right, Clarisse?"

The man was a charmer. Back in the day…

"No comment. Sienna, we'll look around at everything—and there's a lot to see, I promise you. Annie, Steve—we'll just head on in, if you'll excuse us. Come on, your mom will catch up."

"Bye, Mama!" Not even a whimper of remorse as she skipped up the steps to the brick building.

Leaving two adults standing on a street corner looking like a pair of tongue-tied teenagers was one stroke this side of brilliant. The only bad part? Not being around to hear what they said to each other—if they managed to untie their tongues and speak, that is.

Chapter 10

Rehearsing all night what he planned to say when he made the face-to-face with Annie should have primed him for the moment. It didn't. Looking into the dark brown eyes, flecked with gold and so soft a man could lose himself in them, banished all logic from his brain.

It affected other parts of his anatomy, as well. A minor miracle. Before he met Annie, he hadn't had any of those urges in longer than he was prepared to admit. Amazing what an engagement called off due to the best man and bride-to-be's pre-wedding shenanigans could do to a guy. He'd tossed the girl, sold the van that had been rocking when he'd gone knocking, and forced himself to never allow a pretty face—or great ass—to get his engine started.

Until now. Damn, but this woman started him up.

Praise the heavens and all things Jimi Hendrix, she met his gaze—and didn't look down. Feeling like a schoolboy, sporting a semi in broad daylight? Humiliation times ten.

"Hey." Brilliant. Not only was logic gone—so were his communication skills.

Thankfully, Annie still retained hers. Obviously, not as affected by their meeting.

"Nice day."

He gazed at the clear blue sky. Not one cloud in

sight. A perfect day for the beach.

The beach.

"It is," he said. "Listen, about last night—"

She cut him off, shaking her head so hard the leather barrette corralling her curls slipped. She didn't notice, and he didn't dare point it out.

"I acted like a—I don't know…I just…"

He put a hand on her shoulder. Soft, warm—just the way it felt last night.

"No, don't. I shouldn't have come on so strong." He wished the sadness he saw in her eyes wasn't there. He wished he hadn't put it there. "I don't know what happened. It was just easy to talk with you…I felt a connection. I was hoping you felt it, too."

Time stops when waiting on a female. He was sure his heart stopped, or at the very least slowed, in his chest.

Annie pulled her lower lip between her teeth. It was beyond bewitching, watching her choose her words while she worried that plump, pink lip. The sight wasn't doing anything to loosen the crotch of his Levis, that's for sure.

"I think that's why I did the white rabbit thing." Annie smiled, and his heart began to thump beneath his t-shirt again. "I feel a connection, too. It's just…ah, I don't know how to say this, but it's just…"

He squeezed her arm, a gentle touch. It occurred that she might be as affected, but hid it better than he did.

"Too much? Too fast? Too soon?"

She laughed, and the tension between them evaporated, chased to the wind and lost to the sky.

"All of the above, maybe?" He ran his palm down

her arm before pulling it away. Once her skin was free from his, the urge to touch her again was overwhelming. "Too this, too that, too fast?"

She nodded. "Probably a little bit of each. Is that terrible?"

"No, it's cool. I should have held back, I know that. Like I said, you're just so easy to feel connected to, and the moment took over and...hey, I'm sorry I chased you off."

She shrugged, a shy movement that made his breath catch.

Demure and sexy—he never would have thought they could mesh, but the living, breathing proof of it looked up at him with a twinkle in her eyes.

"I shouldn't have run. I feel foolish. Forgive me?"

"If you can forgive me the steamroller act."

"Nothing to forgive." She shook her head, and the barrette finally fell free. He caught it, then held it out. Her fingers brushed his palm as she scooped it up, sending a *zing!* up his spine. "Thanks. I thought something was going on up here."

Running her fingers through her waves, fanning the hair across her shoulders—hell, it was almost painful to watch something so simple yet so mind-numbing.

"Then it seems we're cool. I'm glad."

"Me, too."

A silence. Short, yet it felt like forever.

When his brain engaged, he cleared his throat.

"Listen, I was thinking it's a great night for the beach." He held up a hand. "No, not that way—I mean, do you snorkel? Or scuba dive? I've got a boat, nothing big or fancy, but it's a helluva lot of fun to take out. Even just past the breakers, to swim. Sound like something you'd be willing to try?"

"Yeah, it sounds cool. But tonight? I don't know…"

Uh oh. "Do you have a date?"

A grin. A heart-gripping grin. "Yeah. With my kid. I didn't eat dinner with her last night, remember? We took the jam to the store, left her sleeping. Clarisse had her in bed by the time I got in."

She took a deep breath, then shook her head.

"I can't. As much as I want to say yes—and I do— I just can't bail on her two nights in a row. I mean, look at me now—the absent parent, standing out here while she's in there. I'm sorry, Steve."

He turned, held a hand toward the historical society's steps. They began to walk, avoiding a fresh crush of tourists practically knocking each other down in an effort to get to the large anchor.

"I get that. But how about if we go out later, say after Sienna is in bed? Would that work?"

They'd reached the top step, stood outside the wide glass entrance doors.

"It would. If you don't mind waiting to take the boat out."

"I don't mind. Being on the water at night is one of my favorite things. It is by far the optimal time for mermaid spotting—do you realize that?" He winked, and she giggled—and they were back to where they were before he'd jumped her in the sand.

"I did not." He opened the door for her, and was sorely tempted to go in, too, but stopped at the threshold. The overzealous crap had scared her off last night. A mistake he wasn't going to repeat.

"Okay, then. See you after dinner. Any special

time?"

She considered. "Sienna should be in bed by nine."

"Cool. I'll be by the house just after the clock strikes nine."

"Okay." She turned to walk in. Hesitated. Stopped, and turned around to face him again. "I'm glad we bumped into each other. Really, glad."

"Me, too. Now, go check out the place. Let me know if you find any wayward pirates in there."

****

Any other time, the Lobster Cove Historical Society exhibits would have caught and held Annie's attention. She would have lost track of the passing hours, immersed herself in tales of pirates, smugglers, scientists and pioneers brave enough to settle in a hard environment under tough conditions.

She would have been swept back in time. Lost in another dimension entirely…

Forgotten about Sputnik. Vietnam. The Beatles.

Any other time that's precisely what would have happened once she stepped into the large brick building filled to the brim with images of days gone by.

But with Steve's voice ringing in her ears, she could barely concentrate. On anything. Or anyone. Including poor Sienna.

Thankfully, Clarisse was in her glory, regaling them with long, involved, intriguing tales. She knew every bit of local lore there was to know, and took great pride in passing it on. Even with her mind in the clouds, Annie thought Clarisse's knowledge would make a fantastic book.

She made a mental note to discuss the book idea, sometime when there were just the two of them.

If Clarisse minded her joining the pair and just walking along, quietly, she didn't let it show. Sienna chattered about everything, asked enough questions for a small army and generally filled the hole her mother's lack of conversation left.

Thank God for the kid, Annie thought.

They entered a large room with floor-to-ceiling glass display cases on all four walls and display cabinets in the center as well. In one corner, a large bell stood on a bricked slab. An enormous figure of a woman, carved from wood and still retaining some of what she assumed was its original paint, hung from the ceiling.

"Neato!" Sienna's head tipped so far back she was nearly doubled over.

"She sure is, isn't she? Take a good look now. We've got time. Give the lady her due respect." Clarisse gave them a few minutes to take in the details.

Every wave on the carved woman's head was perfect, and looked windswept from her brow. Her eyes, huge and chocolaty brown, should have seemed blank and staring, but instead were lifelike and mesmerizing. Her clothing, a low-cut, cleavage-barring periwinkle blue dress, hugged a form hinted at in full detail by the masterful carving.

"From a wreck?" Annie knew it had to be, or the female form wouldn't be in this room. She looked around. The cases held bits and pieces…definitely from a wreckage.

So sad. She was so gorgeous and had obviously met a bad end.

"Oh, yes. She's our most famous wreck, actually." Clarisse sighed, gazing lovingly on the figure above them. "Our own Duchess Jane Ainsley."

"You know who she is?" Annie thought it was just some random representation from a woodcarver's imagination.

"Certainly. She was carved in the likeness of the duchess herself. They were both on the ship, aptly named The Duchess, when it sank in eighteen-fourteen Just past the shoals, it was. The real duchess was never recovered. But this washed up on the beach, thankfully. As did the Duke."

"A duke in Lobster Cove? Really?"

Clarisse smiled. "Yes, we had a duke here, Annie. In fact, he liked it so much, he stayed. Buried up near the Methodist Church, he is. I imagine he fell in love with the weather here—why, there's no comparison to the drab English countryside, is there?"

Sienna asked the question Annie knew she would. "What happened to the duchess? I mean, the real duchess?"

Clarisse inhaled. Held it. Then, she exhaled and looked down at the little girl.

"Well, sweetie, that's the thing. Nowadays, we'd say she passed on, was drowned in the sea after the ship crashed. That's how we would explain the disappearance. But in eighteen-fourteen, well, people looked at things differently. They didn't share the opinion we have."

Persistent to the very end, Sienna asked, "So? What did the old Lobster Cove people say happened? Huh?"

"The scuttlebutt—which means gossip—about the Cove was that the duchess didn't drown. They say she became a mermaid."

Chapter 11

Annie had planned how it would be when her date arrived. So smooth. So casual. Laid-back, relaxed, and ready—that was the vision she had.

She wanted to be ready when Steve showed up. Dressed nicely. Hair brushed and styled. Makeup minimal, but pretty. The whole extreme eye shadow and liner, red lips, and heavy rouge was never her thing but clean, a hint of blush, eye makeup, and lip gloss never hurt a woman. Less was more, in her eyes.

That was the plan. But as mothers with small children learn the hard way, plans went awry. Seriously awry.

She groaned when she heard the doorbell chime. Elbow deep in soapy sink water—just the way no woman ever wanted to be found when a date arrived. She grabbed the dishtowel, wiping her hands as she headed through the house.

He stood on the front porch looking as if he'd just sailed off the pages of a Casual Male catalog. Hip huggers slung low, the flare at his ankles neither too wide nor too skimpy. The usual t-shirt had been changed out for a navy blue, Nehru-collar shirt. Untucked. Brown huaraches on his feet. Totally ready for a night at the beach.

Conscious of her wild curls, Mr. Bubble-stained jeans, bare feet, and unadorned face, she smiled. She was aware—painfully so—of a big wet spot on the center of her tie-dyed What's Gnu? t-shirt, proof that she'd been washing dishes and splashed herself on display, but she smiled anyway.

No use acting as if she didn't know she looked a mess.

"I'm running late." Waving a hand down, indicating the dishevelment she couldn't hide. "I'm sorry."

"No big deal. What can I do to help?"

She motioned him inside. As he passed, she caught a whiff of his aftershave. Musk—sexy and masculine, it made her forget how crappy she looked. But—oh, she probably smelled of bubbles, powder and the chili pot she'd been scrubbing.

"Nothing, really. Except maybe give me ten minutes to pull myself together." They headed for the kitchen. She had only been in Clarisse's home for a few days, yet it seemed the natural place to go. The heart of the house. She filled the chili pot with hot water. When she went to lift it from the sink, Steve nudged her aside and picked up the heavy pot.

"Where?"

"On the stove. I'll let it soak overnight." She fitted the lid on the pot, then went and rinsed out the sink. "Can I get you anything? A beer? Soda?"

Steve sat at the kitchen table. Sienna left a Tom and Jerry coloring book open, crayons spread around it. He began to gather the crayons, sticking them back into the Crayola box one at a time. She noticed he put them in carefully, not damaging the points.

"Nothing, thanks." He stopped, looking up with a smile. "Take your time. I may just color—that is, unless you think she'd mind."

Annie grinned. "A coloring kind of guy, are you?"

He'd turned to a fresh picture and surveyed it with a practiced eye. "Nah. Oils are more my thing, but a man's gotta be flexible. Crayola is the next best thing to the paintbrush." He looked up. "I've got a niece and three nephews. I've got lots of coloring experience— but hey, don't spread that around, okay?"

"Your secret's safe with me. Sure I can't get you something?"

Steve smiled, and it seemed the room got brighter. So calm in the face of chaos. He'd come looking for a woman ready to go on a date. Instead he'd found chili-splattered shirts, rioting crayons and Medusa-like hair. And he acted as if it was the most natural thing in the world.

"No, thanks. I'm really fine. And don't hurry. The ocean isn't going anywhere. I'm in no rush, Annie. Let's just take the night as it comes."

"Sounds awesome. Let me get myself cleaned up, then we can head out. And if you change your mind—"

She was about to open the refrigerator and point out the offerings. He shook his head, waving her toward the door.

"Don't worry about me. Believe me, I've been in Clarisse's kitchen many, many times. I can find my way to a bottle of Coke if I get parched. Go on, take care of you. Let the rest of us hang for a while. It's your time."

She didn't need to be told a second time. Letting the fridge door close, she turned and headed for upstairs. Where, hopefully, Sienna would be fast asleep. And Clarisse would be out of the tub. And, finally, she might shine up enough to feel more like a woman and less like a—

Annie stopped halfway up the stairs. It hit her that while she loved being Sienna's mother, suddenly it didn't feel like...well, like enough. All this time, she'd never wanted more than what she had. But now, with wet cotton sticking to her abdomen and her hair in complete disarray, she wanted. And it felt good.

Sighing, she headed for the bathroom. It was, fortunately, empty so she closed the door, stripped out of the messy clothes, and stepped beneath the hot shower spray.

Time for a transformation.

Time to move on. She hummed a bit of Santana's *Oye Como Va* as she shampooed the scent of chili beans from her hair.

****

If she knew how much he'd wanted to lean down and kiss her when she'd opened the door, looking all warm and sexy with that big spot of water making her shirt stick to her like a second skin, she probably would have slammed the door in his face. He hid it, but it hadn't been easy.

The woman did strange things to him, things he didn't try to understand. There was no point, really. Just go with the flow had a nice, peaceful ring to it. And if there was anything the crazy world needed, it was peace.

Clarisse came into the room on bare feet. She looked like Mother Earth herself, in a rust-and-green flowing caftan. Hair held up on top of her head. Makeup free and looking as if the world couldn't get much brighter than it was.

"Steve. I thought I heard the bell."

He stood, then sat when she waved him down.

"Can I get you anything? A cold drink?"

She paused by the refrigerator, but he shook his head so she came to the table and sat in the empty seat beside him. Looking over at the page he'd nearly filled with color, she raised one eyebrow.

"Who knew? A Van Gogh in Lobster Cove? My, what a headline that will make for the morning paper!"

"Shh! It's a secret." He grinned, gave Tom cat's tail a final bit of shading. Putting the crayons back in the box, he admitted, "I had these all put away, but I just couldn't resist giving it a go. Not bad, if I do say so myself."

They looked at the drawing. Tom, the big cat, stood on one side of a wall. Just beyond his sight Jerry, the mouse whose life the cat tried to make as miserable as possible, stood—a huge grin on his little face. Tom, hammer in hand and ready to smash the mouse when he ran out, had no idea a stick of dynamite was tied to his tail.

"Not bad for you. Not so good for the cat." Clarisse pointed to a blank corner. "You should sign it. Tomorrow when Sienna sees it, she'll know you were here."

He chose a blue crayon and signed a corner of the paper with a flourish. Then, he added a sketch of a daisy beneath his name.

"Flower for the sweetie."

"Yes, she is a sweet little girl." Clarisse folded her hands on the table. "And her mother is sweet, as well. Apple trees make apples, you know."

She was getting at something, that was clear. But

rather than try to guess what the riddle meant, he waited. He'd learned with his own grandmother, who regularly played bingo with Clarisse down at the Community Center in the church basement, that when a woman of a certain age had something to say, it was generally best to let it be said in its own time. Probing only made for cryptic answers and confusion. Best to let things take their own course.

Still, a man had to respond when being stared down by the female in charge of the conversation.

"Yes, I suppose they do. Make apples, that is."

He closed the coloring book. Placed the box of crayons on top of it. Folded his own hands on the table. Waited.

Not long, though. Upstairs, the sound of running water stopped.

Clarisse looked at him for a moment. She cleared her throat. "So you're taking Annie out on your boat? Is that the plan?"

"It is. We can go swimming. Or night fishing. Or, we can just watch the moon and stars for a little bit. Whatever she wants," he added. So far, so good. The answer earned him a tight nod.

"That sounds pleasant. Just make sure that woman doesn't come home tonight as rattled as she did last night, Steve." When he opened his mouth to speak, she hoisted a hand and looked away. "No, don't say a word. I don't want to hear it. I don't want to know anything. All I'm saying is, I want Annie and Sienna happy here. The woman who ran up the stairs last night—as if the hounds of hell were on her heels, mind you—wouldn't convince anyone she was happy. Happy women don't dash home from walks on the beach with men."

She paused, letting her words sink in.

It was all true, of course. There was no reason to even try to deny it. That would be a lie, and he wasn't a lying man.

So, he met her gaze. Let Clarisse stare him down. Kept his mouth shut. And waited.

Again, he didn't have a long wait. Footsteps on the floorboards above their heads hurried the conversation to a conclusion.

Clarisse leaned closer and dropped her voice. "I mean it, Steve. I want them happy…so maybe they'll stay in Lobster Cove. And if you can't make that woman happy—well, then back the hell off. Do I make myself clear?"

He smiled. Gave her a nod. In a whisper, he answered, "Crystal clear."

"Good," she whispered back.

"What's going on here? You two have secrets I should be worried about?"

Annie entered the room on a cloud of Tabu. She looked as good as she smelled.

"You polish up beautifully." He stood, walked around the table and took the emerald green sweater hanging from her hand. Draping it around her shoulders, he winked at Clarisse. "Nothing to worry about with us, is there?"

"Nope. Not a thing." Clarisse stood, wiping an imaginary spot off the wooden table with a palm. She gave them a bright smile. "You two go have a great time. If you spot a pirate, bring him home for me. Otherwise, just enjoy the night. It's a beauty."

She walked out onto the back porch, waving as she left. Through the doorway they saw her stand at the edge of the top step and look skyward.

"It is a beauty," he said softly. "And so are you."

Chapter 12

"Watch that board. Big Al came down on it pretty hard Memorial Day weekend. Has a crack the size of the San Andreas Fault. It won't take much to make it cave all the way." Steve took her hand, led her around the dicey plank, and further down the dock.

Glad for the grip he had on her hand in the deepening twilight, she skirted the spot.

"Big Al?"

"Yeah. Big Al. You'll meet him. He runs the bait shop at the end of the dock. That's his day job. By night, he plays the sax down at the Shack."

"The Shack?"

"The Lobster Shack. It's a dive, but we love it. The local hangout; every once in a while a tourist wanders in. but for the most part it's just us townies." They reached slip number twenty-seven; the numeral was painted in day-glow paint on the piling. "We can go there sometime, if you don't mind hanging with the riffraff."

"Riffraff?" She was beginning to feel like a parrot. "Really? In a place like this?"

"No, not really. I was only messing with you." He swept his free arm out, toward the boat bobbing near them. "Here she is. She's no yacht, but hey, I'm no movie mogul."

Annie bit her tongue. Swallowed. "Um…"

He guessed what she held back. "Movie moguls? Just up a ways, there's a busload of them—although I doubt any of them have ever seen a bus, except maybe in one of their movie productions. Yeah, Bar Harbor's becoming Hollywood's summertime playground. There, and Kennebunkport, the beautiful people play. Here, in the Cove, just ordinary folks."

"Nothing wrong with ordinary."

"That's what we tell ourselves." Steve stepped onto the boat, turned and waited. "Just one foot over the railing, a step onto the seat and down in. Easy."

Glad she wore low espadrilles, Annie lifted the hem of her flowing yellow cotton skirt and followed his directions. When she reached the deck, the boat rocked gently beneath her feet. She stood beside him for a few moments, not moving or speaking. Just getting her sea legs.

"Got it? The movement okay for you?"

She moved further onto the boat. A little area behind a windscreen held two chairs. Both, bolted to the bottom of the boat.

"Yeah. I'm fine, thanks."

"Great. Have a seat, and we'll be out of here in a flash." Steve loosened the rope holding the craft to the piling, threw it into the bottom of the boat. and moved to the captain's chair. He put a key into the ignition, turned it, and instantly the boat came alive.

The boards beneath her feet vibrated, making the gentle rocking seem tame by comparison. Steve turned to her and grinned.

"Ready?" His grin made her heart skip a beat.

Words escaped her, so she nodded.

He drove the boat from its slip, past the other boats

tied in place and out into the open water. Free from confines, he turned to her and grinned again, the look pure bad boy.

"Ready now?"

"You know it." Annie laughed at the feeling of sheer freedom as the boat gained speed.

It had been so long since she felt weightless. So long since the burdens of life hadn't held her down. So long since…hell, so long since she'd felt alive.

That was it. Steve made her feel alive.

And it scared the shit out of her.

****

He had wrangled with himself all day long, wondering just how to get close to Annie without frightening her off again. Because even to a simple guy like him, it was obvious that was what had happened. He'd gotten too close, too fast, and she'd run.

Damn, but could she run!

If she bolted now, he'd have to get wet going into the ocean after her. So better not to chase her off.

Neutral conversation. That was the ticket.

Raising his voice to be heard above the roar of the engines, "Shame about that guy. You must have heard—a guy washed up on the beach last night."

"Yeah. Clarisse told me about it this morning, but no one else seemed to know anything more. I wonder what happened." She paused. Blushed. Looked up at him, fluttering eyelashes so long they should be illegal. "For a minute, I thought it might be you. You know, going in search of mermaids or something."

Moonlight danced on her curls, turning the honey to gold. Captivating, and making his fingers itch to run through that silky beauty. He tightened his grip on the wheel.

"Nah, not last night. Not in a long time, actually."

"Glad to hear it. So, I wonder who it was?"

"Some guy named Ken James. That's what I heard, down at the Shack at lunchtime. Poor bastard." He hugged the coastline, moving fast enough that the ride be exciting but not so fast they bounced over every swell and wave.

"What happened? Do you know?"

He reached the lighthouse point. Slowed the engines. Then, angled the craft so it lay parallel to Lobster Point, the jutting pile of rocks that ran from the lighthouse into the ocean.

Steve cut the engine. Waves slapped against the wooden hull, a rhythmic sound he loved. Many times he'd come out here, just to get away from everything. More nights than he could count, he'd fallen asleep at this very spot, listening to the slapping waves.

Swiveling his chair so it faced hers, he was distracted by the way her skin glowed in the moonlight. The skirt, so vibrant and sexy, was topped by a sheer, almost-see-through blouse. The deep vee at the neckline exposed more than a bit of skin—all of it tempting. To run his lips along her neck, down lower…the thoughts that invaded his mind…

What the hell. Take a chance.

Steve leaned forward, placed an arm along the railing beneath the windscreen and dove in.

"I'm sorry I scared you."

Annie took a deep breath. Held it. Then, a slow, sensual exhale. She shrugged, and he peeked into her blouse as it fell open a few inches.

"I shouldn't have been so easily scared." She

sighed. The sound seemed older than she was, and he wondered how so much depth could come from such a petite figure. "I'll be honest...I haven't got a lot of experience with men. I know we're all free-love, post-Woodstock, but I guess I've been out of things."

"Raising a daughter. Alone. That has to take up most of your time. Energy."

"It sure does. I keep men—not that there's a whole line of them or anything—but I keep men pretty far away. Just seems better for my daughter."

"And easier for you, too." He spoke in a low tone, making it more a suggestion than statement. But, she didn't try to deny it.

"You know it."

"Well, I'm still sorry I made you run. That wasn't my intention."

A small smile brought the edge of her lips higher. "Oh no? What was your intention, then?"

A clearer come-on hadn't been invented—so he jumped at the encouragement.

"This..."

The moment his lips touched hers, Steve's body responded. Heat coursed through his veins. The sea breeze couldn't cool the rise in skin temperature that spread out from his core. He reacted to the soft sweep of her tongue against his.

He'd wanted their kiss to be sweet. Friendly. Non-threatening.

But he couldn't hold back. A growl came from somewhere low as he deepened the kiss. Claimed her—even if only for a minute.

Annie hesitated when he palmed her cheek, pulling her closer. It was only a slight hesitation; she moaned softly, pressing her skin against his hand.

If he didn't stop he knew he would go further. He wanted to—hell, how he wanted to.

But if he scared her now, she had nowhere to go. And he wasn't a fan of being trapped, so trapping a woman wasn't anything he was prepared to do.

With a swallowed groan, he broke their kiss. Leaned his forehead against hers for a long, quiet moment. It didn't escape notice that Annie's breathing was rapid. Ragged. She'd been as affected as he'd been.

"Wow," she breathed. A whiff of perfume invaded his head when she shook hers. It was perfectly suited to the woman—irresistible.

"An understatement." He chuckled. Sitting back, he ran a hand through his hair. God, but it was almost impossible to resist leaning back into the woman and kissing her until neither of them could think.

Kiss her senseless, he thought as he plowed his fingers over his scalp a second time.

"I...ah..."

Annie giggled. Just a small giggle, but it was oh, so alluring.

Again, he wanted to grab her and kiss her until his world exploded.

Shit. How could she affect him this way?

"Yeah. I hear you." He looked for a safe topic, one that wouldn't make him want to take her in his arms and throw her down on the floorboards. "So—what were we talking about?"

"Ah...oh, right...um, the body. The man who came ashore. I wondered if anyone knows what happened. You know, why he was in the ocean, why he washed up on the beach."

A safer topic.

"Draft dodger, apparently. Poor bastard was trying to elude Uncle Sam, swimming from who-knows-where for we'll-never-know now. His luck ran out, I guess. Or he didn't swim well enough to get where he wanted to be. All I know is Audie, the police chief, came into the Shack for his usual crab cake sandwich and let it spill that the draft dodger was on a slab at the county medical examiner's office."

Annie's face hardened at the explanation. Another woman might have looked ugly, with furrowed brow and thin stare. Or, the rosebud mouth set in a straight line would detract from beauty. But not this woman—if anything, the stern expression, all no-nonsense schoolmarm if ever he'd seen one made her even more attractive. The soft lines dulled, bringing a dimension that he realized lay just beneath the surface. So close, yet out of reach.

Her words shocked him.

"Got what he deserved, then." No hint of compassion, not even the tiniest shred, for the dead man.

"Really? You really feel the guy deserved to die for standing up for what he believed in?"

Annie sat back in the seat. A sharp nod.

"Definitely. Thousands of men are fighting a war—dying for what America believes in. Anyone who can't see that is…is—shit, anyone who can't see fighting with his brothers in arms is a privilege, is a coward. And cowards? They get what they deserve. Plain and simple."

For a moment, he felt nauseous.

The night he'd envisioned was as dead as the poor

guy down at the coroner's office. So, Steve stood and went to the wheel.

Starting the engine and turning the boat around gave him something to do, which was good since he couldn't find one single, solitary thing to say in response to the woman who'd just cut him off at the knees.

At least he knew where he stood with her. Or didn't stand.

Chapter 13

Dust motes flew through the air, dancing in the sunbeams coming through the open doorway. Sienna sneezed. Once. Twice. The third one was the loudest, and brought a small exclamation with it.

"Oh crud!" She turned, running a finger beneath her nose and scowling at the air. "How can anybody breathe in a place like this? Too many dust thingies!"

Clarisse had been counting jars of jam in a far corner of the shop. Without turning around, she said, "There's a dust cloth under the counter. If you want the dust thingies to scram, you could chase them out. Give the place a good dusting, child."

Annie stood on a ladder, replacing burnt-out light bulbs. It had been her suggestion that they come down to the shop and tidy it up a bit. She'd woken up restless—and confused. A distraction, such as dealing with the empty place, was just the thing to take her mind off stuff.

She watched Sienna walk through the aisles, toward the checkout counter. The store was old-fashioned, laid out with shoulder-high shelving forming two wide aisles, leaving the remainder open. Countertops and tables were used for display in the open area. Along two side walls, glass display cabinets, so old the oak frames held wavery glass panes.

Pulling a dust rag out from under the cash

register—a near-antique, itself—Sienna stood. Waved the rag in the air.

"This?"

Clarisse glanced up. "That's it." She made a fast notation on the legal pad by her side. "Just wipe it along the tables and shelves. Gather up the dust on the rag. And when you think you've got some dust, go on over to the door and shake it outside. That would be a huge help. Don't you agree, Annie?"

"Completely. Honey, with you doing that, we'll get the place spiffed up much more quickly. And once we're done here, I thought you might want to go to the beach."

The child's squeal of excitement filled the space. Clarisse's shoulders went up, but she smiled as broadly as Sienna did. They watched the little girl dance in the aisle, twirling so rapidly her pigtails flew out from her head.

Sheer pleasure, Annie thought. It's awesome, that my baby girl is so happy here she dances just for the sheer pleasure of it.

She couldn't be doing everything wrong. Even though it sometimes felt that way.

"Really? The beach?"

"Unless you don't want to go..."

"Nooo..."

"No? Oh, that's fine. Clarisse and I will go then—just for a little while, since you're not interested..."

She heard Clarisse's stifled chuckle.

She also heard her daughter's loud reply.

"No! Mama, you can't do that!"

"But you said—"

Sienna flapped the dust rag in front of her face,

gathering dust motes from the air. With her red Keds, short denim overalls, and striped t-shirt, she looked cuter than cute. Annie marveled that the little person stomping one foot for emphasis as she cut her off was hers.

If she lived to be a hundred, the miracle of having Sienna would never fade.

"I said yes! You guys can't go without me—that's not groovy."

Annie unscrewed the last brown bulb from the light fixture. She replaced it with a new sixty-watt bulb and climbed down the ladder. Tossing the bad bulb in the garbage, she shook her head.

"Did you hear that? Not groovy, Clarisse."

The older woman clucked her tongue against her teeth. "I hear. Not groovy." She noted a figure on the pad, tucked her pencil behind her left ear and looked up. Meeting Annie's gaze, she added, "But between us, I've never been a groovy sort of…oh, what do you call it? Hen? Duck?"

Sienna burst out laughing. She clutched her belly and doubled over. "Chick! A groovy chick!"

Clarisse winked over the child's head.

"Well, that, too. So if I go to the beach with you ladies, will I be a groovy chicken then?"

If Sienna laughed much harder, she might wet her pants. Annie hadn't brought a change of clothes for the kid, so she put the stops to the funfest.

"Hey, groovy laughing girl, you should get to that dusting. The faster we get things squared away here, the faster we get to the beach. Understand?"

Sienna sucked in a deep breath. She wiped her streaming eyes with the dust rag. "Yeah. But it's groovy chick, not chicken!"

"Duly noted," Clarisse replied.

Sienna headed for the counter closest to the open door. Then, she poked her head into the sunshine, lifting her face so the sun warmed it. She closed her eyes.

"Mama? I'm gonna get the windows out here first. They need dusting, too."

She walked outdoors. Putting the rag to good use, she began to wipe the window glass where she could reach.

"Looks like we're going to have one clean stripe at the bottom of that window." She looked at Clarisse, who had finished counting jam and moved on to the maple syrup bottles. "I hope you don't mind."

"Not at all. Why, this place needs sprucing up, even if it's just one stripe at a time." Clarisse looked up from the bottles. She turned, put a hip against the shelf behind her. Crossed her arms.

Always a lady, even in white pedal pushers, white ankle-tie sandals and navy blue sleeveless cotton blouse, the elderly woman perused the empty space with a shrewd eye. Annie had the feeling she saw the place as it had once been rather than how it stood now.

Her hunch proved correct.

"Back in the day, we could hardly keep these shelves stocked. I know it must be hard for you to believe, but it's true. Why, as soon as the place opened we'd get the early crowd. You know, the ones who came in for odds and ends to make breakfast or pack a lunch to take to the beach."

"I believe it. I can almost hear the footsteps shuffling on the floorboards and voices comparing varieties of jam for their toast. Oh, it's easy to see this place must have been bustling."

"It was." Clarisse reached a finger toward a shelf, flicked a bit of dust off. She wiped her fingers together before she continued. "Like I said, we couldn't put stuff out fast enough. By lunchtime, we had a full house. People buying home-baked bread and pies—which I made, every night after closing. Salads for the beach—macaroni and potato salad were big. Egg salad, too—for sandwiches. And drinks, they sold well. We never sold the hard stuff—you know, liquor—but we did sell some beer. Just two brands, I think—Ballantine and Schaeffer's—because George favored both."

Annie heard the wistful turn to the woman's voice when she mentioned her husband. It was a tone she understood all too well.

"You miss him."

Clarisse nodded. "Of course. I'll always miss him. But that's not the only thing I miss."

She waited. It had only been a few days, but they had already learned each other's nuances and styles of communication. The relationship forming between them was growing exponentially, a bond that felt completely right.

The older woman met Annie's gaze. Unshed tears shimmered in her gray eyes.

"I miss the store, too. I miss being here. Talking with customers. I miss baking pies and bread. Oh, I miss it all, I suppose. It was an amazing time in my life—the best time in my life, and I just miss it all. Not only George—although he's a huge part of it—but the whole adventure. It's as if my life is over...yet I'm still living. The fun is gone. Done. Finished...yet I'm not.

Does that make any sense?"

"It makes a lot of sense." Annie swallowed around the lump that had formed in her throat without her even feeling it. "I...wow." She shook her head, trying to assemble the jumble of thoughts filling her mind into some kind of order.

A deep breath. This was supposed to take her mind off last night, off the confusion of having been unceremoniously dumped at the curb outside the house with hardly a "goodbye" from her date. Instead, she still had the mystery of Steve to deal with...along with the feelings stirred up by Clarisse's admission.

The truth. It was the only way to go, and she knew it.

"I understand." She met Clarisse's gaze, this time knowing it was her own eyes that held the sheen of unshed tears. "I understand because I feel the same way. I miss someone—and will always miss him. But, I miss the carefree, fun days that came before all hell broke loose. I miss the way I used to be. I'm not the same person, and I miss that. I...oh, hell..."

The tears fell, sliding silently down her cheeks.

Clarisse stepped closer. Put her arms around Annie's shoulders and pulled her tight. It felt good to be comforted, rather than comforting, for a change, so she leaned into the other woman and made no effort to squelch the tears.

Stroking her hair with a slow hand, Clarisse waited until the worst of it was over.

"It is all right, I think, to miss what is gone. But—and here is where I sometimes stumble—it's not all right to lose yourself wishing for what's gone, and ignoring what could be. The heart only moves on when it realizes it can't go back, my dear. I think we both have to send the message to our hearts...we need to move forward. Become groovy chicks instead of wishing-for-the-past turkeys."

Annie swallowed, just as Sienna poked her head in the door and hollered, "Hey, are we ready to go to the beach yet?"

"Are we ready, Annie?" Clarisse asked. "For the beach...and everything else?"

She drew in a deep breath. Then, she nodded. Turning to face her daughter, the biggest reason for her to face forward and find a happy future, she smiled.

Annie grabbed Clarisse's hand. They went to the doorway, and she grabbed Sienna's hand as well.

Looking from one to the other, she asked, "Well? What are we waiting for? Three groovy chicks— heading for the beach. Let's go!"

Chapter 14

"Mind telling me what crawled up your ass and died, man? Don't remember ever seeing you this down."

Big Al wasn't known for his finesse. Or his sense of style.

Steve looked up from the lunch special he'd been choking down.

The large man himself stood beside Steve's table. The Shack was pretty full, but there were seats at the bar so Big Al's interruption was purely intentional. Wearing his usual frayed blue jeans, faded t-shirt and untied sneakers, he waited patiently for an answer. Not replying wasn't an option.

"Nice to see you, too."

Steve pushed his dish back. Damn, but his appetite had blown off on the wind.

Big Al didn't wait for an invitation to join him. He pulled the wooden chair on the opposite side of the table out, the wobbly legs screeching against worn linoleum floor, and sat heavily. Pushing his sweat-stained, wide-brimmed hat back on his head, he stared.

Shit. The guy wasn't giving up. And he didn't feel like playing thirty questions.

"So? What is it you've got up there, buddy?"

"If I say it's none of your business?"

Gwen, with her waist-length brown braid and on

near-silent feet in brown suede moccasins, stopped by the table. The waitress never carried an order pad. Her mind was, she loved to say, like a steel trap. Whatever that meant.

"What's it gonna be, Big Man?"

Big Man. Just one of many monikers—as if "Big Al" wasn't enough.

"Ah, the usual, I guess. A crab cake sandwich. Fries. Onion rings. And chocolate milkshake."

He hadn't gotten to be Big by birth.

Gwen saluted smartly, turned, and went to the kitchen to put in his order.

Like a dog with a bone, the man was on his back.

"So? You gonna spill it—or am I gonna hafta drag it from you?"

Steve sighed. He and Big Al had been friends for longer than he could remember. They'd shared high school football games. Dating local girls who only used them for movie admissions, leaving them for the rich guys from Bar Harbor as soon as they'd eaten the popcorn. And Steve had been around when Big Al's wife had lost her battle to the big C. Damn, but a beautiful young girl shouldn't endure suffering like Jess had.

If he was going to spill his guts to anyone, Big Al was a likely candidate.

"Chick."

One word. Explanation delivered.

"Oh, man…that's tough. Sorry to hear it."

"Yeah, well…what are you gonna do? Shit happens, right?"

The meal arrived. Steve hadn't touched his. Big Al sent a pointed look at the plate.

"You've got to eat." He raised his sandwich, took a huge bite and began to chew. He swallowed, then raised an eyebrow. "I mean it. Dying of starvation isn't going to make the chick deal any better. Eat."

Maybe food in his stomach would stop the pain in his head. Steve took a bite of the cold sandwich. It wasn't awful, so he chewed.

"I didn't know you were going out with anyone. Who is she—and where did you meet a girl in this place? Seems like we've been dating the same chicks for years, man. Is she someone I know?"

Steve hesitated. Big Al was right. They'd all dated the same people since high school. It got old, real old, a long time ago. A way long time ago. Suppose the guy inhaling the crab sandwich across the table decided to make a play for Annie?

Annie. Just thinking of her made his gut clench.

Why hold back? It was for damn sure she wouldn't be interested in him when she found out the truth. No way. No how.

"How'd I meet her? Let's just say we scraped fenders."

"What?" Big Al moved on to the onion rings. Watching the man eat was like witnessing a train wreck. Too interesting to look away, but kind of hard to see close up. He was like one of those high-power vacuum cleaners used for sucking up leaves in the fall. Anything within range of the guy's mouth disappeared—fast.

"I was backing out, she was driving through. She hit my Harley with her Barracuda."

"A hit and run, eh?"

"You could say that." He took another chunk out of

his crab cake. Now that he'd begun, it went down pretty smooth. "No real damage. Just a couple of scratches that'll sand out easy."

Big Al grinned. He waved a French fry in the air. "So—more love tap than fender bender?"

"You could say that."

"So? What's the deal? She pissed over her Cuda's scratch?"

Steve shook his head. "Nope. That ain't it. She's not pissed over anything—yet."

Polishing off the fries, Big Al raised a questioning brow. He looked at his watch, then met Steve's gaze. "Spill it. If she's not pissed—yet—how can you have chick troubles? Don't sound like you've got any troubles, man."

Steve shoved the last of the sandwich in his mouth. He pushed his plate toward the center of the table, which was all the invitation his dining companion required. Big Al stuffed two now-cold fries into his mouth and chewed, giving him enough time to consider his reply.

He was a simple kind of guy. No pretensions. No mystery. So, he just laid it bare.

"The guy who washed up? The draft dodger?"

"Yeah—so what?"

"Our newcomer seems big on the go-to-'Nam bit. She's kind of happy the guy drank the sea—says anyone who's not ready to march off to this bullshit war doesn't deserve to live. And that, my friend, is why I know I've got chick problems."

Big Al stopped chewing. He gave a low, soft whistle as he shook his head. When he looked up, the truth showed on his wide face.

"Shit. I'm sorry, man. That blows."

"Don't I know it."

****

Clarisse had waited as long as she could. Everyone expected that just because she was old, she was wise. Calm. Patient. Well, everyone could go jump rope—she'd had enough waiting for Annie to tell her what was on her mind. Time to find a crack in the vault.

Sienna played down at the water's edge. A hot pink-and-white two-piece bathing suit kept her visible. Not that there was a crowd for her to blend into. Wednesday afternoon wasn't prime beach time for most. And, the tourist season would be in full swing by next weekend. The fourth of July festivities was the first real heavy traffic, beach-wise.

They sat on an old, patchwork quilt. She took a swig from her cold bottle of Fanta orange soda. Swallowed. It went down fast on such a hot day.

"You're kind of quiet." An unthreatening beginning to any conversation. Hoping to not put Annie on the defensive, she added, "Is everything all right?"

Annie took her own sip of soda. She spoke, looking at the bottle she rolled between her palms.

"I don't know. I mean, I don't think so. Well, maybe." A huge sigh. She scowled at her bare, pink-toenail-polished toes. "Oh, shit." Looked up, zoning in on her daughter. Then, "Really, just shit."

Clarisse chuckled. She'd felt that way about too many things to let a little swearing bother her.

"Well, damn it, dear—what's the matter?"

Annie turned and met her gaze, a tiny grin pulling her features into a vision. There was something about this woman, something that wasn't at all ordinary or common. Once again, she gave her grandson credit for finding, and recognizing, such a treasure.

"You did not just say that!"

"Oh, but I did." Clarisse watched as Sienna began chattering with another little girl. About her age, and wearing a one-piece bathing suit that was an almost exact match to the hot pink Sienna wore. "You can't think that I'm so ancient I have forgotten how to swear. Damn it all to hell, my dear…goodness, but I hope I'm never so senile that I forget to talk like a sailor when the need arises."

She gave Annie's shoulder a gentle poke, glad that the connection they'd made encouraged such closeness. It had been so long since she'd felt connected to anyone. So long since she'd felt comfortable enough to speak so freely.

She could get used to all of it—being with people she loved and sharing good moments. Making new memories. Especially, watching the little girl grow.

"I hope someday I'm half as amazing as you are, Clarisse. Really, you're a role model—I love it that you do what you want. Say what you mean. Tell it like it is."

Annie sighed again.

"Your turn to tell it like it is." Annie gave her a sideways glance, so she nodded and said, "Really. Get it off your chest. Whatever's bothering you—it's like an upset belly, better out than in. So, let it out."

Spreading her hands wide, sloshing the half-bottle of soda she held in her right hand, Annie said, "I don't know. I thought Steve and I were having a great time last night. We walked to the pier. Talked. Laughed. Got on his boat. It was a gorgeous night—stars like you can't even imagine, just twinkling over our heads. It seemed…"

She waited. One minute. Two.

"It seemed what, Annie?"

"Perfect."

She waited again.

"We kissed, and it was perfect…but…"

"But what?"

"He stopped. And when Steve looked like he might kiss me again…well, there was only one time, but it was there. You know, the look in a man's eyes when he's considering making a move." She shrugged. "I waited. Maybe I misread him. We talked. He looked like he was going to kiss me some more. And then…"

Damn it, but the suspense could kill an old woman! And, Sienna and her new friend were saying their goodbyes. If she didn't get the end of the story now, she might never get it.

"And then what? What happened?"

Annie looked up when Sienna called to them. She glanced at Clarisse and shook her head.

"Nothing happened. That's just it. I thought he liked me…but then, he just brought me home. And no goodnight kiss, either. I-I…I don't know. Maybe I misread him."

"Maybe he's an idiot," Clarisse said, under her breath.

Chapter 15

"Mama, can I use this one? It really should be colored. White is so square."

Annie looked up. Her daughter, all hip lingo and colt-like legs, stood on the back steps. Waving in the small sea breeze, and dangling from one finger, a white halter top. It was barely a month old, bought at a roadside sale on their trip north. It had never been worn, and had its original tags still attached. On the one hand, she hated to see a perfectly good shirt subjected to a dubious outcome. On the other, encouraging Sienna's creative urge was worth the price of a shirt. Especially when the shirt had only set her back two quarters.

"Where'd you hear that word?"

"From the guy on the television. Last night."

Annie had gone for a long, quiet, thoughtful walk last night after dinner, leaving Sienna with Clarisse. She hoped Clarisse hadn't let her daughter watch the nightly news report. While she wasn't a fan of the square box, she let the kid watch certain things, like Happy Days. The news broadcast was the only thing she felt strongly enough about to ban from Sienna's sight. Too much violence, stirring too many memories.

"The commercial guy. You know, the Apple Jacks commercial. Mama, can we get some Apple Jacks? There's a prize in the box that looks pretty good."

Grocery shopping with Sienna usually meant

boycotting the cereal aisle. As well as the cookie aisle. And the candy aisle. There wasn't room in the budget for extras, particularly extras loaded with sugar and ingredients whose names she couldn't pronounce.

"We'll see."

"So maybe on the Apple Jacks and yes on the shirt?"

"Right. So we've got the socks, the t-shirts, and baby dolls. Is that it?"

"My shirt." Sienna skipped across the lawn and tossed the shirt onto the pile of clothing slated for the dye baths.

Annie had already mixed dye, water and vinegar in five aluminum buckets she'd found in the garden shed. Once hosed off and de-bugged, they were ideal containers for their little project. Clarisse hadn't seemed to mind that her grass might be psychedelic for a while after they were finished. She'd given her blessing before heading off to the Historical Society.

She didn't think she'd forgotten anything. They both were wearing last year's bathing suits, so even if they were careless and splashed dye around, they should be able to come clean. And not ruin anything, a primary objective. Sienna's creative gusto usually meant something suffered.

Pointing to the pile of rubber bands and string, she said, "First, we twist the fabric. Remember, you can make designs—kind of, anyhow—with the rubber bands and string. Wherever the rubber bands are, the dye won't be, so that part will stay white."

They sat cross-legged in the grass. A t-shirt, soft from washing, twisted easily into shape. She pulled a bit into a tight circle, secured the bundle of fabric with a rubber band, and then held it up.

"See? If we make little bundles all over this shirt, it will come out with lots of tie-dyed circles on it. Cool, huh?"

Sienna nodded. She grabbed a shirt, pulling it onto her lap and concentrating on bunching the fabric into place. She wound a rubber band onto it, then looked up.

"Cool. But can you show me how to make a heart?"

Oh boy. It figured her kid couldn't be content with circles. Hearts? She almost said it couldn't be done, but the expectant eyes staring up at her stilled the words on her lips.

"A heart? Hmm, let's see…"

She pushed and twisted, coaxing the cotton to cooperate. When she secured the rubber band, she said, "I think that might just do it. Not a hundred percent sure about it, but maybe. It's the best I can do, honey."

Sienna fingered the misshapen bump in the fabric. With a grin, she said, "It'll work. Now let's make more. All over everything. Hearts and hearts and hearts…"

By the time all the hearts that could be fit onto any space on all of their items had been made, dyed, rinsed and hung to dry, they were both covered in subdued blotches of red, yellow, green, purple and blue.

Sienna pointed toward Annie's midsection. The tiny green bikini, with its heart cutout on the left breast cup near the frayed tie string and low, side-tie bottoms, left a lot of room for wearing the dye. She looked down at the riot of color on her tanned stomach.

It was pretty similar to the splatter covering her daughter's exposed belly.

They looked at each other and giggled.

"We dyed ourselves too, didn't we?"

"Pretty neat, the colored tummies." Sienna licked a finger, traced a heart on her skin and giggled harder. "You can't change it, Mama. Look, the heart disappears into the blue!"

A fast rub on her own sun-warmed, dye-splotched stomach confirmed her suspicion. They might be tie-dyed for a few days, if not a week.

"How about if we disappear beneath the lawn sprinkler? Maybe that'll get some of it off."

Annie positioned the sprinkler far enough from the house's open windows and the newly dyed apparel hanging from the clothes line that nothing would get soaked. She walked to the side of the house, turned on the spigot, and adjusted the water's height. The day was warm, and it took no coaching at all to get the child beneath the spray. She watched for a few minutes, knowing that while the day was hot, the water was cold.

Still, the longer she let the dye soak into her pores, the less likely it was to wash off. She took a deep breath, ran across the yard and into the sprinkler water.

Sienna laughed, throwing her head back to the sky. Annie's heart swelled. The child was so beautiful, such a gift and a tangible reminder that she had loved—even if only for a short time. Water dropped onto her daughter's closed eyes, hanging from the thick brown eyelashes for a scant second before sluicing down her cheeks. The summer sun had brought a sprinkling of freckles across the bridge of Sienna's nose. Annie wanted to lean down and kiss each one.

Instead she held out her hands. Motioning Sienna closer, she said, "Come on, let's get that bathing suit top off. Then you can really get some of the dye off your neck and chest."

The backyard's fencing and tall trees made a secluded oasis. She had no worry that anyone from the street could see her half-naked child. Besides, nudity was natural.

The string on the wet bathing suit didn't untie easily, but she managed to get it off. When she did, Sienna used the fabric like a washcloth, scrubbing at her blued knees and green arms.

Using her palms to splash the water across her body got some of the color off. Most remained. Her daughter seemed to be having a better time of it, scrubbing the dye off with the bathing suit top.

Annie looked around. They were alone.

She reached behind her neck, undid the clasp holding her suit in place. She did the same at her back, caught the fabric in her hand and took her cue from the child.

Sienna didn't bat an eye. They'd showered together before, so this impromptu bit of backyard baring-it-all didn't faze her one bit.

"Like this, Mama. You kind of rub hard in one spot and it disappears." Pointing to one pink-rather-than-red knee, she added, "Well, almost. But it's better, don't you think?"

"Sure is. I don't know how we got so dyed, Baby Girl." The endearment elicited a grin from Sienna. She scrubbed at her own knee, bending from the waist. "We dyed shirts, socks and us, it seems."

"It was fun. And, I like the hearts. Don't you?"

They stood, angling their bodies so the water hit them in the back, and looked at the things drying in the sun. Covered with irregularly-shaped hearts, the clothing had turned out better than Annie hoped. It wouldn't sell like hotcakes in a big department store, but she was pretty certain that if she pursued this tiny flicker of an idea that had invaded her brain somewhere during the previous long, restless night, she might be able to make a few bucks selling to tourists.

She'd envisioned circles. Sunbursts radiating out from the centers of simple t-shirts. Maybe coordinating socks. Never hearts—leave it to her big-hearted child to think of that.

"I do. Very much. It's awesome that you thought of hearts. I wasn't going to make anything that seemed complicated. But it wasn't, not really."

"We just tied them up and out came hearts." The words simplified the process the way only a child can do. "Now that we know how to do it, can we make more?"

She looked down at the stains on her fingertips. Making a living wasn't meant to be white-glove clean.

"We can. That's the idea, actually. I'm thinking that we might go into business, making tie-dye shirts and stuff to sell. What do you think of the idea?"

"We're not gonna sell those, are we?" Sienna squinted at the things they'd created. "Those are ours, right?"

Annie put a hand on the wet head. She let her fingers trail through the dripping curls.

"Right. Those are ours, but I think we'll make more. Like I said, maybe to sell."

"Okey dokey. I like that. But Mama, I'm hungry."

"Well, let's get rinsed up and go inside. I bet there's enough strawberry jam for two big fat sandwiches."

They turned back to the water sprinkler. Sienna was so intent on scrubbing up and getting to lunch, she didn't realize they weren't alone. But Annie did.

Steve stood at the corner of the house.

Chapter 16

In a pintsized place like Lobster Cove, avoiding someone was no simple task. Steve felt like a boxer, ducking and dodging, trying to anticipate where the three females living on Elm Street might be at any time of the day. It wasn't just Annie he avoided. He didn't want to see any of them—not even the kid. Hell, no.

Not after he'd seen so much of the mother. And damn, but what he'd seen had been…man, it made him hotter than sand on the beach in July just thinking about it. Some things couldn't be unseen once they'd been seen. This was one of them—thank God.

He had a feeling Annie wouldn't think his sightseeing moment was as much a lifetime highlight as he did. She had to be pissed. The look in her eyes when she turned and caught him in the yard—hell, yeah. She was pissed.

Two nights ago, after he'd peeked around the corner of Clarisse's house, he took a long, long walk on the beach. After a few—okay, maybe more than a few—beers at The Shack. Big Al had tried to engage him in conversation, but Steve kept what was on his mind—and affecting the state of his jeans—to himself. The last thing he needed was to have the whole town know the war widow had great assets…and was showing them off for free.

Every year the town cop dealt with a couple of

nude sunbathers. They were all used to that, out-of-towners and city people looking to let it all hang out, regardless of who had to see it. Nudity? Part of life, but he was still kind of old-fashioned and figured the lady in his life should keep her skin to herself unless they were alone.

But hell, he didn't have a lady in his life, did he? Wishing he did didn't make it so.

The first night? Beer. Beach. And, finally, falling asleep on the boulders at the north end of the dunes. He hadn't slept there since he was in junior high. Back then, the rocks hadn't seemed so hard. He'd woken stiff, sore, and hungover.

Last night he'd gone home—with a six-pack of Schaeffer's to keep him company. If he'd only killed the six, he'd be fine. But the fridge held another two—and they put the ache in his head when morning hit.

It made fixing the missing shingles on Cora Weston's florist shop—in the midday sun—a challenge. But he'd managed, and also managed to avoid Cora's none-too-subtle overtures. Since her husband had left her for another woman, she was hot to trot. If town gossip was to be believed, a number of men had already "trotted" with the woman. He, however, had no intention of being one of her stabled suitors.

The shingles had blown off in last fall's nor'easter, toward the back side of the building. His perch concealed him from passersby below on Main Street, and that was exactly what he planned. No one could speak with him unless they were willing to climb a ladder and walk across a hot shingle roof.

He could only hide for so long. It was becoming tedious, and it was only a measly couple of days. How anyone went into permanent hiding was beyond him.

It was cooler off the roof. He stood beside the ladder for a long moment.

Climbing on his bike and heading out of town had crossed Steve's mind more than once. The feeling of freedom on the road? The antidote to the trapped, nowhere-to-hide situation he'd backed himself into.

But, he'd never run from anything. And starting now—because really, that's what it was, running—wasn't something he was prepared to do.

The feel of the bike beneath him never grew old. He'd tinkered with engines all his life. The roar of a well-tuned machine was almost as satisfying as the moan of a well-loved woman.

Steve pushed the thought of being above any woman out of his mind, and rode down Main Street. Playing cat and mouse had to end. He was tired of being the mouse.

Lobster Heaven was hardly heaven, but it was the best they had. Ronnie Murray had owned the store since his dad passed on, just after they'd graduated high school. Since he'd been deployed, his wife Rachel and sister Norah ran the place. Lucky for Ronnie, the two women had some business sense. If he was lucky enough to come home from 'Nam in one piece, he'd have a business to fall back into. And if he came back to Lobster Cove in a box, the way four others already had, his wife wouldn't be lost wondering what to do without him.

Steve pulled into a space in front of the shop. Cut the engine. Kicked the bike into position. Then, he swung a leg over and stood on the sidewalk for a minute.

Tourist season had hit. Good for the economy. Crap for locals who loved the peace and quiet of a place off the beaten track, like him.

Sighing, Steve turned and headed for the open door. Strains of Hendrix met his ears. Low, but there. The place was empty, just Norah stocking shelves. She looked up at the sound of his footsteps on the wide-plank flooring.

"Hey, how's it going?" Norah was a year younger, a year behind him and Ronnie in school. Back then, she'd had a crush on his brother's friend. Now, she was engaged to a guy from Bar Harbor. He, too, was somewhere far away, fighting people they had no quarrel with, probably in a village no one stateside could pronounce.

He smiled as she stood. All legs, Ronnie's sister. If he'd had half a brain in high school, he'd have made time for her. But that was then, this was now—and he hadn't been smart enough to see the potential behind his friend's little sister's mooning over him.

"Good. And you? How're things?"

She shrugged. The halo-wearing lobster logo stretched tight across her breasts as her blue t-shirt moved with her shoulders.

"Not bad, I guess. Still no news…not in three weeks or so. Nothing from Ronnie. Nothing from Jimmy." Norah fiddled with the package of wood screws in her hands. The galvanized metal inside the sealed box tinkled with every movement.

He searched for a reply, then settled on the obvious.

"No news is good news, right? That's what they say, anyway."

Norah met his gaze. He saw fear in the soft gray eyes. She forced a smile. It was transparent, but at least she tried.

"That's right. No news is good...that's what they say...whoever the hell 'they' are." A ginger curl fell across Norah's shoulder when she shook her head. "Ever wonder who the all-knowing 'they' really are?"

He'd never, but he nodded. "All the time. All the freaking time."

She held up the screws. "Need something else for the roof?"

"Nah, thanks. Done up there."

The shop sold mostly lobster traps and supplies for fishing boats. The stainless and galvanized materials that worked well on the sea also held up well on exterior repair jobs. The shelves were stocked with a wide assortment of household, building and fishing repair odds and ends. Ronnie's dad had known what people wanted, and Lobster Heaven still gave it to them.

A teasing tone. "How'd it go with Cora? Hmm?"

Easy to not kiss and tell when there were no kisses. "I fixed her roof. That's it."

"Just her roof?"

"Just her roof."

"Well, you're the only guy since Woodstock who got away from the place without attending to any of her other needs. I always heard Gary loved it that she has an eye for other guys—gave him more time to kick back and smoke."

Gary had never bought a Marlboro in his life, but he'd been the go-to guy for some grass if one was so inclined. Neither had killed him, although everyone in town pretty much figured he'd been high when he'd stood behind his pick-up truck by the side of the road one night after drinking too many beers on his way home from work. Moral of that story? Put the brake on before taking a leak—unless you want to go with a drunk smile on your face and your pecker in your hand.

"Yeah, well, I just fixed her roof. And hasn't Gary been the butt of enough jokes already? Let's leave the poor guy in peace, okay?"

"Peace, man." She flashed him the two-finger sign. "Just chewing the fat, no need to wig out."

He raised his hands. "No wigging. Just saying—all I know is I wouldn't want people talking about me the way we talk about him. We need to cut the guy some slack—and maybe his widow, too."

"Gotcha. So, if it's not roofing supplies, what can I get for you?" She placed the box on the shelf beside her shoulder.

"I need some more of that low-luster polish for my boat. Did the order come in yet?"

Norah walked to the wooden counter near the door. She slipped around it, and he noticed that she'd lost weight. War was hard, not only on those in combat but the ones left home, as well. It seemed to be taking a toll on Ronnie's sister. Steve wondered if he should ask her out to dinner, or even just a cup of java or a beer at The Shack. She sure looked as if she needed some chill time.

"You're in luck. It arrived last night, and I remembered you were looking for some last week so I put a can aside for you. Jack Parker wanted as much as I have for his skiff, but I held back. Only for you, Steve." She reached down, then brought a sealed can from beneath the cash register. It hit the countertop with a dull thud. "Anything else?"

Steve reached into his pocket for some cash. "Nope. That'll do me."

"Five even. No tax. Believe me, I love a day when I can take a little from Uncle Sam—after all he's taken from us." She accepted the five dollar bill, punched a key on the register, and slapped it into the cash drawer when it opened. Norah shut the drawer with her hip.

"I hear you. Listen, though, you've got to keep your chin up. Ronnie would expect that. And your dude, well, I'm sure he would, too."

She nodded, a resigned movement. The curl swung beside her face, free from the bandana holding her ponytail in place.

Impulse won. Steve reached out, pushing her hair off her cheek with the tip of one finger. Her skin was soft and warm beneath his skin. The movement didn't seem to startle Norah, so he let his finger linger. She leaned into his touch, so he opened his palm and held her cheek.

Tears shone, unshed, in her eyes. He swallowed around the sudden lump in his throat. God, it must be hell to wonder where someone you loved was. What they were doing. How they were eating and sleeping. And whether or not someone was shooting at them. Bombing them. Covering them in the heinous Agent Orange cloud.

It was a miracle women could tolerate any of it without going insane. He was pretty sure he couldn't carry on as if the war wasn't happening if someone he loved was over there.

"Listen, Norah…"

Words failed him. A tear glistened on one eyelash; he was sure she didn't even know it was there. He brushed his thumb across it, slow and gentle. The moisture clung to his skin.

In another lifetime, he could have fallen for her. But the love shining in her eyes told the truth: Ronnie's sister wasn't so little anymore. And, she was head over heels in love with the guy who probably tramped through the rice fields with a submachine gun this very minute.

"It's okay. Really…no one knows what to say. What to do." She shrugged again, and again the t-shirt went from casual to traffic-stopping. "I get it. Everyone's afraid they won't come home in one piece. I'm afraid, too."

He didn't insult her by saying it wasn't so. A small shrug, one sweep of fingertip across creamy complexion. It was the most comfort he could offer, the best he could do—and it was damn little, he knew that.

"Hey, when do you get out of here?"

"Six. You know that, silly. You and Ronnie used to count the minutes in the last hour, remember? At six—not five after, but exactly six—he'd lock the door so you two degenerates could grab a beer at The Shack. You didn't forget, did you?"

"I didn't forget." He took a deep breath, and offered something he hoped would be seen as it was intended, a simple between-friends gesture. "Listen, would you like to go for a ride on my bike tonight? After you're done here? Maybe catch a bite to eat? It just seems…hell, Norah, it just seems like you need a shoulder and damn it, Ronnie would expect me to offer mine to his sister. Strictly old friends passing some time. What do you say?"

Norah hesitated, so he pulled his hand away. Grabbing the can of polish, he said, "You don't have to answer now. Let me know later, okay?"

He turned toward the door. As fate would have it, the woman he'd been striving to avoid stood in the doorway. She held Sienna's hand and looked like a deer caught in the headlights of a semi. Had he not spotted her, he figured she would have turned and left.

"Uh…"

Brilliant move. Now his tongue was glued to the roof of his mouth.

Luckily for Annie, her tongue worked just fine. She shot him a cool look.

"Hello."

He swallowed. "Hey." A good time to make an exit.

With a smile at Sienna, Steve attempted to walk around the two females but was brought up short by the sound of Norah's voice.

"Steve—I can tell you now. I'd love to take a motorcycle ride tonight. Dinner sounds excellent, too. So, I'll see you at six, then?"

What could he do?

Meeting Norah's gaze and completely avoiding Annie's, he answered, "Six. On the dot."

Then, he got the hell out of there. Fast.

Chapter 17

If looks could kill, he'd be dead so he counted himself lucky—if being the damn unluckiest guy in town could be called lucky. Shit—he sure could get himself neck deep in the stuff without even trying. All he'd wanted to do was something nice for an old buddy's sister, and it'd bit him right on the ass.

That should teach him. No more Mr. Nice Guy.

Until next time.

Steve stepped out into the street, not bothering to look up from the pavement, and got a blast from old Mrs. Gorman's Caddy horn. Actually, the hulking, shiny black beast was her departed husband's vehicle. She'd been denied the privilege of driving it while Mr. Gorman was alive. Now that he'd taken his leave and rested in the town cemetery, Mrs. Gorman drove like the bat out of hell her old man had feared lived within her.

He held an apologetic hand up, waving at the woman. She stuck her left hand, burning Marlboro dangling from arthritic fingers, out the window as she blasted him one more time with the horn.

The old lady had balls. He'd give her that much. She had to be at least seventy, and drove the car as well as any Saturday night drag racer. He'd barely cleared the front chrome bumper when she gassed it, maneuvering around him with just inches between his butt and all that chrome.

Damn, but women were strange creatures. If he lived to be a hundred—and he sure as hell hoped he wouldn't—he'd never fully understand that half of the human race.

Only one thing to do when backed into such a tight spot.

He checked his watch. The Shack should be open, or at least opening. He wasn't hungry for lunch yet, but a nice, cold beer would do just fine about now. And the bonus of not being in the company of a female for a half-hour or so was just icing on the cake. Highly unlikely he'd even have to speak to anyone, which suited him just fine.

Like a guided missile, Steve headed for the pier and the burger joint.

****

"Why didn't Steve say hi? He saw us, Mama. I know he did."

Sienna swung the small brown paper bag wide, narrowly missing smacking an elderly woman walking on the sidewalk. Annie motioned for her to tone it down, and the child did, making her motion less enthusiastic—but still wide enough the handful of clothespins inside made a satisfying noise.

Annie wasn't in the habit of lying to her kid, but the occasional fib, especially when it meant she wouldn't have to explain the stickiest situation she'd been in since their arrival in Lobster Cove, didn't seem like a bad option.

"I don't know."

She took Sienna's hand, then they crossed the street. Traffic was busier than usual. Tourist trade, probably. And it was interesting that she'd only been in town a short time and already felt attached enough to think of anything being unusual.

Maybe they'd found a place to call home. She wasn't entirely convinced yet, but between Sienna's happiness and Clarisse's nightly persuasive, over tea or sangria talks she was beginning to feel swayed to stay. For a while, anyhow.

They reached the other side and blended into foot traffic. Clusters of shoppers meandered, browsing storefront displays and examining sidewalk sale items. A cloud of menthol smoke washed over her, and for an instant she wished she hadn't given up the habit last year. It had taken her through the early widow days, the moments she wasn't cuddling her baby and didn't know what to do with her hands. A cigarette seemed a better option than wringing a tissue. It was hard to cry when smoking, so even though the habit had cost her it was cheaper than getting soused on homemade wine, the way some other war widows did. She'd never taken to smoking pot, either, even though a number of other widows at the support group she'd attended a few times extolled the virtues of weed.

No, her primary commitment was to her baby, and being stoned or drunk wouldn't make her the kind of competent parent she knew she could be. So, she'd smoked Newports, until she realized they, too, were only a crutch. And one she could hardly afford.

But that didn't mean that every now and then she'd love a drag off a cig… Being human had its faults, and this was one of hers.

"You know he saw us. He could've said something. He didn't ask me to ride on his motorcycle—"

"You are not riding on any motorcycles, so put that right out of your head. Come on, Clarisse is probably already waiting for us."

The idea to get out of the house and discuss their "options", as Clarisse had been calling the thread of possibility they'd been tossing about, was a good one. And since Sienna had been begging to see the inside of The Shack since she'd spotted it the day they drove into town it seemed as good a place as any to meet for lunch. Clarisse's morning at the Historical Society had her up and out before either of her two housemates were awake.

The no-motorcycle scowl that she'd been on the verge of receiving melted as they walked up to the front of the eatery. Annie opened the door, and her daughter skipped into the place, her steps matching the beat of Creedence's *Who'll Stop the Rain?*

Clarisse had chosen the table closest to the water's edge. Small boats bobbed along the pier, and others wound in and out of their spots as they docked or left for the sea. Better than television, the comings and goings should keep the little girl occupied enough that the adults could speak without interruption.

Annie had been counting her blessings since moving to Lobster Cove. Clarisse was an incredible woman. Sienna was happier than she'd ever been. And here there was hope for a firm future, something she hadn't expected to find.

"Hey, chickie, how're you doing?" Clarisse held her cheek out and smiled when it was kissed. Sienna slid around the woman's chair, plopped her sack on the table and sat in the chair closest to the wall of glass.

She put her hand on Clarisse's arm, and it crossed Annie's mind that the pair looked like they'd known each other forever.

"I'm good. Cap'n Crunch for breakfast. And we got clips for the shirts at the store."

"Sounds like a bang-up morning. Let's see those clothespins." Sienna opened the bag and they peeked inside. The older woman nodded her approval, and the child closed the bag and deposited it back on the table beside her paper placemat. "Just what you need to make more shirts. Too bad I don't have enough, but they couldn't be too pricey, could they?"

Annie answered. "Just a buck. And these are to replace the ones we used. You can't hang your laundry with tie-dyed clothespins."

"A small price to pay to see our business take off."

A waitress appeared beside the table. No note pad, Annie noticed.

"Good to see you, Clarisse. It's been a while." A snap of bright pink bubblegum punctuated the greeting.

"You too. Yes, it gets pretty busy around now, as you well know. And I've had family come to live at the house, so we've been having fun getting better acquainted. This is Annie, my grandson Brian's widow, and their daughter Sienna."

Annie felt the other woman's appraisal as they exchanged hellos. Then, "I'm sorry for your loss. The fighting?"

Annie sighed. Was there anything else that would kill a perfectly healthy man in this day and age other than that damned war?

"Thanks. And yes, he was shot in Cambodia."

"Happening to too many good guys over there.

What a damn shame."

"It is." Annie hated the small talk, as if reducing the carnage to a couple of murmured platitudes might make it somehow better.

Fortunately, Sienna had been perusing the menu on her placemat. She interrupted and for once Annie didn't bother to correct her.

"Chocolate milkshakes—Mama can I have one with my grilled cheese?"

"Yes, you may. And do you want French fries or onion rings?" On the drive north they'd stopped at a roadside diner and Sienna had discovered a love for batter dipped and fried onion rings.

"Rings!"

The waitress smiled. "I'll make sure you get a big order, honey. You look like you have a taste for them. Me, too."

Clarisse shrugged. "Make that two, please."

Annie looked up at the woman who waited for her order.

"What the heck? Might as well make that three."

When the waitress left, Clarisse steepled her fingers and took a deep breath. She let it out slowly, then said, "So. I stopped into the shop before my shift at the Society. I think that with a few alterations—and minimal ones, at that—we can turn the place into something new. Keep some of the old, but make space for the things we're mulling over. A few dowels from that far wall will let us hang things. And the display shelves will hold any kind of merchandise. Not a big thing, even with a little bit of painting, to clean the old place up."

A jolt of excitement shot through Annie's center. It

was a big step, agreeing to reopen the shop with Clarisse. It meant she planned to stay for longer than she'd initially thought. It meant spending the summer, at least. And, probably, the fall also. Sienna had to be enrolled in school somewhere…why not Lobster Cove?

A parade of "what ifs" sped through her mind.

"What if—"

Clarisse cut her off. Apparently what worked well for a child worked equally well for a senior because Annie's mouth snapped shut.

"We're not reinventing the wheel, Annie. If we can't sell things to the tourists—who are just itching to spend some of their cash, if I may add—we can't sell things to anyone. Really, it's just a matter of giving people what they want. That's all we need to do. Now, are you in?"

She drew a breath larger and deeper than the one Clarisse had drawn just minutes before.

Then, she took a leap.

"I'm in."

The die was cast. No turning back, no disappointing an old woman. Just forward movement, and hopefully fuller savings accounts for both of them.

Clarisse slapped her hand on the table.

"Done! I hoped you would agree!" A smile stretched her facial features, pulling some of the wrinkles out and giving a glimpse of a younger version of herself. She must have been a stunner back in the day. "Now, all we need to do is get someone over there to do the heavy stuff. I think we can do most of the painting, don't you?"

"Definitely."

Their lunches arrived. The food looked amazing,

and the scent of the fried onions made her mouth water. Sienna dug right in, popping an onion in her mouth, then fanning a hand in front of her lips.

"Hot!"

"Of course they are. Here, drink some of your shake."

They waited for the child's face to turn from bright red back to its normal suntanned glow before they began to eat. The food was simple but tasty. They ate in silence for a while.

When Clarisse swallowed the last of the first half of her sandwich, she wiped her fingers on the paper napkin in her lap.

She nodded toward the far end of the room. "I'll talk with Steve. He's right over there."

Annie choked on an onion ring. Her eyes watered, and she was sure her nose was running. Struggling for air, she gasped, "Where?"

"Goodness, don't take on so. Swallow—and here, have some milkshake. It cures everything, doesn't it, Sienna?"

They watched while she composed herself. Drying her eyes, she said, "You mean he's here?"

Clarisse resumed eating. Nonchalant, but with a gleam in her eyes.

"Mm hm. He's been here since before you walked in. You missed seeing him but boy, oh boy, he didn't miss seeing you. He's been looking this way the whole time. Can't keep his eyes off you, actually."

She could imagine what he saw when he looked at her. Her cheeks heated at the memory of standing topless while he stared.

Clarisse said, "Although I'm kind of annoyed with

him, to tell the truth. He was supposed to stop by the house the other evening."

Her windpipe nearly closed a second time. "The other evening?"

"I asked him to go in the backyard and take a look at my shed. It needs gutters."

He'd gotten more than he bargained for. And at least there was a reason for his presence—he wasn't just a low-life voyeur. That made it somehow better.

Clarisse went on. "But he didn't show, apparently. And he hasn't been in contact. But that's about to change, my dear. I'm going over there and ask him what's up. And, I'm going to tell him we need some work done at the shop. We can't open the place until it's spruced up—so let's get on the sprucing."

Chapter 18

"You're gonna rub the wood down to nothing, man. That boat couldn't shine any more if you dipped her in that varnish." Big Al settled himself on the piling, an act of precision given that his anatomy was considerably larger than the wood he sat upon. But he managed, with a small grunt and a bit of wiggling, to place himself within scowling distance.

Steve tossed the polishing rag onto the deck. He rubbed his hands down the back of his cut-offs and stared at the spot he'd been working on. The wood was mirror shined.

Big Al was right.

He sat on the sun-warmed starboard leather bench seat.

"I'm an idiot." Steve plowed his fingers through his hair. It was long, hitting low on his collar. His fingers splayed the curls, then he slapped his hand on his cheek. Palming his face, he realized he hadn't shaved in a while. The stubble was past the prickly stage, and onto feeling soft.

The last time his face had seen a razor was the night he took Annie out. The night he'd meant to make history with that smart, sexy mama. The night that had turned to shit faster than a heartbeat.

Damn, but his life sucked.

"Nah, you're not an idiot." Big Al carried a bottle

of Coke in one beefy hand. He took a swig. Burped. "You're just a guy who fell for a pretty face. It happens."

"She's more than a face, man. Much more."

Raising the bottle in salute, he belched again. "Figured you'd say that. You've got it bad. Real bad. Any man can fall for a piece of ass—hell, we've all done it—but you're gone on the whole package. There's only two ways to deal with something like this."

Since his father's death, and with all the guys his own age off fighting in 'Nam, Steve had no real friends or confidantes. Sure, he knew everyone in town, but that didn't mean he wanted to hear what they thought about anything of real importance. Idle chitchat? Fine. Life-altering advice? No way.

Big Al was the best he had.

"Two options? Do a guy a favor and lay them out, if you don't mind, because I'm just not seeing them. I feel…" How to admit he didn't know how he felt? That this topsy-turvy mind trip was all new to him?

"Forget it. Doesn't matter how you say you feel, all that counts is how you react to what you think you feel. So yeah, there's only two ways through this."

That struck a chord. His father quoted Winston Churchill whenever he felt Steve needed a push. Now, the line, and his dad's voice, filled his head.

"The only way out is through. My dad said that—a quote from Churchill."

Big Al snorted. Finished the Coke and bent nearly double to put the empty on the wooden pier. He straightened, wiped his brow and said, "A helluva guy, your dad. Churchill, too. But your father was right—

and that makes my point even stronger." He folded his hands across his stomach, his palms covering the straining fabric. "Like I said, two ways out. First, you can get your ass over there and work this out with the pretty lady. Whole town's talking about her and Clarisse opening that old shop again. By this weekend, I hear. She's over there now, painting the walls in a teeny-tiny pair of hot pants and one of those skin-tight midriff shirts." He placed a hand over his heart and fluttered the fingertips. "Damn near gave me a heart attack watching her bend over to refill that paint brush."

A picture flashed through Steve's mind. He pushed it away—fast. That ripe body had been in his head and dreams for days now, and adding fuel to the already-smoldering fire wasn't going to do him any good.

"And the other option?"

Big Al shrugged. "Beat it outta town. Get on that shiny bike of yours and hit the road. Just give in, man. She's outta your league, or maybe you're too afraid to see if you've got what it takes to get a chick like that to fall for a dude like you. I dunno…it's your call. But if you're scrubbing a hole in the hull of this boat, you've either gotta make a move or leave. It'd be a damn shame to kill a perfectly innocent boat just because you're too chicken to go after what you want."

Shit. The fat guy didn't pull any punches. No, he hit Steve's Achilles heel, without worrying about the fallout.

Being the only healthy-looking man left in town, the only one not off serving his country, made walking the sidewalks very difficult. He knew the truth, even though he hated it. And he knew most everyone knew why he wasn't carrying a rifle and wearing camouflage, but whether or not the good people of Lobster Cove believed the reason why he wasn't doing battle was a whole other story. He looked fine. Why wouldn't they assume he was fine?

And that left only one logical reason for his being the only "able-bodied" man in a town left bare of testosterone.

He had to be a coward. A chicken. Lily-livered.

His heart hammered in his chest. It beat fast and hard, like something caged seeking release.

Taking a deep breath, Steve stood and stepped onto the seat. One leg over the side, onto the pier. Then, the other. He met the other man's gaze.

"I'm no chicken."

"I know that. Now, go act like the man we both know you are. Go talk with that woman. Tell it like it is, man. If she's who you think she is, she'll accept it. If she doesn't…well, it's best to find out now if she's just another cutie in hot pants."

****

Sweat dripped down the side of Annie's neck. A single wet line crossed her collarbone, slid into the round collar of her shirt and lower, between her breasts. Her hair, pulled into an untidy heap on the top of her head, was damp. Even the shorts felt sticky, and they were only a thin layer of white cotton.

When she insisted she'd paint the shop, she had no idea that painting could be such hard, sweaty work. Even if she had, she wouldn't have given in to Clarisse's idea they ask Steve to do it.

The temperatures had risen steadily all week, turning the pleasant ocean breezes into steaming bursts of hot air. The first scorcher of the season had hit with a vengeance. Locals predicted it would end soon, probably with a bone-shaking thunderstorm.

Annie was ready for thunder and lightning. It had to be better than this walking-through-hell heat.

"Hey."

The voice. She knew it.

The shop's doors were wide open, to let in any little breeze and chase out the paint fumes. Evidently he'd made use of the open-door policy.

She sucked in a breath and turned to face him. Steve stood just inside the doorway, hands in pockets of tight jean shorts. His Woodstock t-shirt was holey, giving peeks at the muscular abdomen that it hid.

Staring at him felt foolish. "Hey. We're...ah, we're not open yet."

Steve's gaze canvassed the space. Shelves had been washed and polished. Windows shone and the lingering scent of Clarisse's special vinegar cleanser mingled with Dutch Boy number 43—Springtime Yellow. The cheery paint, subdued but uplifting, made it look twice its size. All in all, the week's progress worked like a charm on a place abandoned for so long. There was no evidence of neglect now, only the possibility of something new and exciting.

They still had a long way to go to get everything ready before the weekend, though.

"Place looks great. You've done a lot of work." Steve looked around, bending to peer beneath the open display counter on the far side of the room. He met her gaze. "Your little helper? She's not a painter?"

"She's at the house with Clarisse. It's too hot, and the day will be too long, to keep her here with me. Besides, I think those two have a blast on their own.

They're probably eating ice cream for lunch or doing macramé on the porch in their bathing suits—"

Bathing suits—the last time she'd worn hers, he'd gotten an eyeful. Annie swallowed her words. Her cheeks grew hot.

If he noticed, he pretended he didn't. Steve cleared his throat.

"Listen, I think it's probably good she's not here. I need to talk with you."

He waited. When she didn't reply, he went on.

"Look, I know I've been behaving like…well, like a jerk. I dropped you like a hot potato last week. Avoided you all this week. And, I, ah…the other night, at the house…"

"I know Clarisse asked you to stop by. I didn't know it then, but she did tell me later…after you, um…you know."

He raised an eyebrow and nodded appreciatively as one edge of his upper lip lifted at the corner. A to-die-for expression if ever there was one. Annie bit her tongue. Better to stand quietly while a man was busy apologizing—and appreciating.

"Right…so, you know I'm not a Peeping Tom. That's a step in the right direction, at least. I didn't know you'd be there. If I did I wouldn't have just shown up that way. Actually, I expected the place to be empty—that's the impression I got when I was asked to check out the work and come up with an estimate."

Annie was sure Clarisse wasn't beyond a bit of matchmaking so she believed him.

"But that's not why I'm here."

"Why are you here, Steve? You made it clear the other night that you couldn't wait to get away from me.

And in the store—well, what you do is your own business but it's obvious you already have someone in your life."

"Norah is my best friend Ronnie's little sister. Ronnie is away, over in the fighting, and I just thought it would be good for her to get out and have some fun. Her boyfriend—excuse me, fiancé—is over there too. And, no one's heard from either of them in about a month." He took a deep breath, letting it out slowly as he shrugged. "That's what that was, with Norah. Nothing more."

"I'm sorry about your friend. Maybe he's just in a spot where they can't get mail out yet."

"That's what we're hoping."

Annie's stomach dropped, thinking about all the men who were, even at this very minute, dying horrible deaths. Images shot through her head, images she struggled daily to keep at bay. The lump in her throat, so familiar these days, made speaking difficult.

She met his gaze, knowing full well her eyes glistened.

"Why, then? Why are you here? So Norah's a friend's kid sister—that still doesn't erase the fact that you cut our date short without any explanation. And I'm an idiot, because I thought the night was going really well. I was having a nice time with you. The moonlight, conversation, wine, boat…it was great. And then, just like that, it ended. So why? Why are you here?"

Her head felt strange. Maybe it was the heat. Or the paint fumes. Or the reminder of what a shitty world they lived in, where good men died for no good reason. Was there ever a good reason to die? She didn't know…but the fogginess creeping into her mind made thinking almost impossible.

Maybe she should have had something to eat before heading out to paint. Maybe…

Crap. Maybe Steve would just leave already so she could sit down before she made a fool of herself.

"You're right, it was great. Beyond great, even."

He plowed his fingers through his hair, and she noticed, not for the first time, that the waves fell naturally into place. Such an appealing package—except that he didn't feel the same way about her…

"So why, then? Why did you turn it off so fast? What the hell happened?"

More importantly, what the hell was happening? Annie put the paintbrush down on a nearby shelf. The yellow would leave a smear on the wood, but she didn't care.

"What happened? I-I—shit, I saw how you reacted to the news about the guy washing up on the beach. I realized that you would feel the same disdain for me when you learned the truth. I—hell, I just figured it was better to…I don't know…"

"What truth?"

The words felt fuzzy in her mouth. It was hard to talk with a tongue that felt fat. She rubbed it against her teeth, hoping to make it return to its normal size but it didn't help.

"The truth about why I'm not in Vietnam. About why I'm the only guy here under the age of fifty besides Big Al. The truth that will probably make you hate me."

"Hate you? Why would you say something like that?"

Were her words slurred or was she imagining it?

"Yeah, hate me. Your husband fought, and here I am, doing odd jobs and trying to atone for my being let off the hook. I hate it—don't you get it? I hate it, and sometimes I hate myself, too. So why would you not hate me when I tell you I'm not fighting this freaking war like everyone else because snooty Bar Harbor doctors say I can't?"

She scrunched up her face, trying to make sense of his explanation. He'd lost her in the jumble of hates and war talk, but the doctor bit really messed with her head. Annie let her gaze drop, gave him a slow, penetrating assessment. Broad chest. Wide shoulders. Killer abs leading into tight denim…her gaze lingered. Then, she forced herself to go lower to the muscular thighs and down to the feet before she swept back up and met his stare.

"You can't come up with a better story than that? Do I look like a fool? Steve, you're the perfect specimen of a man if ever there was one! I don't know why you're not fighting—I hadn't given it much thought, really—but trying to say that's the reason for treating me like Hanoi Jane…well, couldn't you come up with something better? Something…something believable…something…oh…"

The floor came up so quickly Annie didn't have time to react before the world went black.

Chapter 19

Annie crumbled like a house of cards in a stiff breeze. Her eyes rolled back in her head, her knees buckled, and before he could cross the ten feet separating them, she went down. The dull thud as she whacked her head on the side of one wooden display cabinet was one of the most frightening sounds he'd ever heard.

The paintbrush had fallen on top of her, landing wetly on the front of Annie's shirt. He pushed it off, his hand sweeping across her left breast. Pulling her body up from the waist, he wondered for an instant if it were wrong to move her. But the desire to tug her close, check her over and wake her threw caution to the wind.

Her breath was strong and steady. He put a finger on her neck, checking for a pulse the way they did on Marcus Welby, MD but all he felt was soft, warm skin. Clammy, but no pulse. Steve laid his hand on the center of Annie's chest, between her breasts. The steady thump of her heart was reassuring. He pulled his hand away, not because he wanted to but because he knew it was the right thing to do. If he had his way, his hand and head would lay up against the woman in his arms for a long, long time without ever moving.

Now what? Putting her back on the floor, even to call for help, was out of the question. Watching her fall had been hard enough. Putting her into the prone position again? Something he couldn't do, not in the shop, anyway.

His bed? Now that was a whole other option… He'd lay her prone on his mattress any day of the week. Any day.

Steve wondered if he should loosen her clothing. On television the guy who passed out always had a tie loosened, but Annie wasn't wearing a tie. In fact, she was wearing very little. Just the tiny top and skimpy shorts. Up close, he realized she wasn't wearing a bra, even. The white top wasn't totally sheer, but it was light enough that her nipples showed plainly through the fabric.

He was only a man. It never occurred to him not to enjoy the sight of those two coral-colored tips poking at the filmy cotton. He'd always been more an ass and legs guy but that could change. Annie's breasts were an invitation to fondle and stroke. He wondered what she sounded like when she climaxed. Was she silent, keeping her pleasure to herself? Or more vocal, giving the man in her bed a blow-by-blow?

His body reacted. The heat in his gut spread lower, moving to places that hadn't been used much in a while. All the no-commitment stuff was great in theory, but Steve wasn't the kind of guy to have nameless encounters with women he didn't plan to see again. The erection pushing against the buttons on his cut offs throbbed, reminding him of its long solitary confinement.

"Enjoying yourself?" Her voice was soft.

There was no use denying he'd been ogling her while she lay out cold in his arms, so he didn't try. He just hoped to hell his cock would get the hint that now was not a good time to be calling attention to itself.

Steve met her gaze. Her eyes looked fine, if a bit sleepy. The pupils were normal, and the look she gave him wasn't fuzzy, the way it had been just before she'd gone down.

He gave her a slow, small grin. "Not the way I generally get a woman in my arms, I'll tell you that much."

One eyebrow shot up.

Good, so she was with it. Still, better to keep her from jumping to her feet, so Steve shifted slightly, trying not to poke her with his crotch while he moved. He lowered his butt to the floor, bent his knees, and made himself into a human chair so she could be comfortable, and a bit more elevated.

Annie looked in no hurry to move, settling her back against his inner thigh. His skin brushed hers, which did absolutely nothing to diminish the party in his pants.

"I bet it's not your best move. You've probably got some smooth moves, don't you, Steve?"

He chuckled, loving it that she grinned up at him.

"Oh yeah, I've got women falling at my feet right and left. I can hardly walk, there're so many chicks passed out in front of me."

Annie shook her head, grimacing slightly. "I did not fall at your feet."

"Yeah, you did. But that hurts, doesn't it?"

A lump, small but unmistakable, grew on her left temple. He pressed it gently with two fingertips. She moaned and pulled away.

"Ouch. What'd I hit, anyway?"

The nearest hospital was in Bar Harbor. He didn't

mind running Annie over there, but taking her on his bike would be dangerous, given the fact she could swoon again at any time.

"The cabinet. Pretty hard, to get a bump like that."

"Why didn't you catch me?"

"I tried, but I didn't get here fast enough." Now he really felt like shit. "Sorry."

She put a hand on the side of her head, but managed a weak smile. "Don't be. I was only teasing you. Believe me, I'm way past the point where I expect anyone to catch me. If I'm falling, I'm either going down or catching myself. That's the story of my life, I'm afraid. Damn, this hurts."

There was no good reply to the statement, although it tore at his heart. No one should feel so alone that they didn't have anyone to rely on...easy to think for someone else when he was pretty much in the same lonely, self-sufficient boat.

Before he moved her, he had to ask. "Does anything else hurt?"

She shook her head, then scowled. "No. Just my head."

"It hurts a lot, doesn't it?"

"I hate to be a crybaby, but yeah, it does."

"Let's get you moved over to the wall. Just a couple of inches, so you can lean back." Annie's slight figure was a cinch to move. When he was sure she was propped up against the wall and not likely to fall over, he held out a hand. "Your car keys."

Her eyes rounded. She stopped rubbing her temple. "What?"

He knew it was going to be a challenge. "I need your car keys. It's not out front, so I assume you parked in the back lot. I'm going to bring it around. Then we're going to get you into the car and over to the hospital." When Annie opened her mouth to protest, he cut her off. "Just to be checked out, Annie. You smacked your head pretty hard—we should let a doctor take a look and make sure you're not hurt more than we know."

"But I don't like hospitals." Her voice was soft, and sad. "I hate them, really."

The look in her eyes said there was more to the story than just not liking the setting but now wasn't the time to ask. They all had skeletons in their closets, things that made them fearful and incited nightmares. Hospitals had to be right up there with killer clowns and snarling monsters on the universal list of fears.

"We need to go." He paused, then added, "And you won't be alone. I'll be right there—that is, unless you want me to call Clarisse to be with you. I understand if you don't want me."

Annie didn't answer right away. When she shook her head, it was a subtle movement. He noticed the swelling on her temple had increased. This was not the time for lengthy discussions; she needed medical attention.

Thankfully, she didn't make a fuss.

"No, please don't call Clarisse. I…I don't want Sienna near a hospital. And I don't want either of them to worry." She swallowed hard. Her eyes shone when she met his gaze. "But I don't think I can get there. I-I…I don't think I can drive. My head is screaming."

He almost laughed at the absurdity of the statement. She was in no condition to walk, let alone get behind the wheel of a car.

"You're not going to drive. I am. Now, where are

your keys so I can bring the car around?"

A tear slid down Annie's cheek. It was almost unbelievable that something so tiny could tear into a guy's heart so hard.

"No one's ever driven the 'Cuda before except me and…"

Steve wasn't a praying kind of guy. Hell, he wasn't even sure a higher power existed, despite the Irish Catholic upbringing he'd had. But if saying a prayer would help get this beautiful woman to cooperate…desperation breeds strange habits. He prayed. Then, he smiled.

"I figured as much." His gaze swept the lump on her head, which was turning purple at a rapid rate. "Hey, what's your husband's name? I don't think you ever told me."

She gave him a heart-melting smile. "Brian. His name was Brian."

"Look, I know this must be hard for you, but we need to get you to a doctor. I promise you that if you trust me, I'll get you there in one piece. Nothing bad will happen if you trust me with the keys. I give you my word, I will take care of Brian's car…and his wife."

Annie closed her eyes. She pointed toward the counter behind him.

"Over there. Next to my purse. You'd better grab that, too."

Chapter 20

Annie felt her head. Gingerly. Sucked in a breath. So, it hadn't been a dream. The tender ping-pong ball attached to her temple was real.

She looked across the bedroom to where her daughter slept. No Sienna. The child's chore list included making her own bed, so it was pulled together haphazardly. She probably had been trying to be quiet, so the finished product was less tidy than usual, but at least it had been done.

A smile crept across her face. Sienna was a good girl. A blessing. Being a mother was the toughest job in the world, but she loved every minute of it—even the messiest, noisiest, most frustrating ones.

Closing her eyes to the sunlight streaming in through the window, Annie stretched. Wiggled her toes. Flexed her spine. It had been weeks since the yoga ritual she'd followed since Brian's deployment had fit into her schedule. In the beginning she had practiced the poses to keep limber for childbirth. Then, following Sienna's arrival, yoga had soothed her frayed nerves and calmed her broken spirit.

She had been so busy with Clarisse and Sienna that she'd let her routine lapse. Now, she felt tighter than she had in years. What was the old wives' tale about the caregiver being excellent at caring for others but the best at neglecting herself?

Ugh. She'd become a fulfilled prediction. How ordinary…

Maybe today she would begin yoga practice again. Nothing difficult, just a few beginner poses to get back into the swing of things. Downward Facing Dog. Cobra. Tree pose.

Before Annie could consider further, the bedroom door opened a crack. A doorknob-height head poked into the room. Following a split second later, an inquisitive face at adult height.

"She's awake!" Sienna pushed the door open further, exposing Clarisse carrying a breakfast tray.

"She is, indeed." Clarisse placed the tray on the bedside table, then turned and probed Annie's gaze with her own. "How are you feeling?"

Her hand lifted, then stopped partway to her temple. Annie mustered a smile of her own as she pulled the little girl who crawled onto the bed close to her side.

"Okay, I guess."

"Hmmph." A cup of tea passed from Clarisse's hand to hers. "Drink this. Chamomile. I know it's not Maxwell House, but you can have that later. First, the tea…I'm hoping it'll chase some of the fuzzies from your head, honey."

Clarisse walked across the room and brought the dainty white chair from the desk to the bedside. She sat and watched while Annie took a first mouthful.

The tea was hot, and sweet, and made her sigh. A wonderful way to come awake. She smiled her thanks and took another mouthful before setting the cup back onto its saucer on the tray. Sitting back, she wove her fingers in Sienna's hair.

"How's my little one today? I'm sorry I didn't see you before you went to sleep last night."

"It's okay, Mama. Grammy told me what happened. I wish I could've gone to the harbor with you and Steve, though. Did you look at boats after you got your head checked?"

Sienna's chatter came at its usual fast pace. Unfortunately, Annie's mind didn't react in its usual equally rapid pace. She struggled to order her thoughts.

She shook her head—which was a huge mistake. The room swam, and her stomach lurched.

"Lay back against the pillows." Clarisse rose, then sat lightly on the edge of the bed. A gentle push pressed her backward. "Take a deep breath and just hold still."

"Mama? Mama, are you—"

She found her daughter's hand. Gave a quick squeeze. She would have tried to answer, but the older woman beat her to it.

"She's fine, honey. Just a tad under the weather, that's all." Clarisse raised a questioning eyebrow, and Annie telegraphed with her eyes that the spinning room was slowing. Turning her attention on the frightened child, she went on. "Your mama and Steve didn't see boats in a harbor. They went to Bar Harbor, to the hospital so the doctors could check things out. See the bump on your mother's head? That will probably pain her for a bit, but she'll get better in a few days."

Sienna peered at the lump. She squinted, bending close. Annie felt breath on her cheek so she mustered a small smile.

Her daughter met her gaze. As solemnly as if she were delivering the nightly news, she said, "That is the most purpley bump I ever saw." Shifting her gaze to

Clarisse, she asked, "Is Mama's brain trying to get out of her head? 'Cause that's what it looks like, you know."

Annie didn't even try not to giggle. She tugged her baby girl close and tried not to flinch when Sienna bumped her shoulder—which set the room spinning again.

"It does look that way, doesn't it?" Clarisse leaned closer, peering intently at the questionable lump. "Hmm..."

When Sienna drew in a frightened breath, a time-worn hand reached out and patted the child's shoulder.

"I'm just teasing. Really, it does look as if something's trying to get out of that pretty head, but it's just a bump. Your mother hit her head. The doctors call something like this, a bump on the head, a concussion. It's a big word that means a person's got a big headache after getting a little bump on their head. We'll take good care of your mother, and in a few days we'll hardly remember this happened. Right, Annie?"

Swallowing hard, she nodded. Meeting Sienna's gaze, she gave her the no-kidding-I'm-your-mom-you-better-believe-me look.

"Hey, when I feel better maybe the three of us can go to Bar Harbor to see the sights. Not the hospital—that wasn't much fun—but to the harbor, if there is one. And I'm sure there's an ice cream shop there somewhere. And, we need a couple of things for the grand opening—maybe we can pick that stuff up then, too. What do you say?"

"There's a big Woolworth's in Bar Harbor. I'm certain we could get the odds and ends we're looking for there..." Clarisse tapped a thoughtful finger against her chin. She pursed her lips, raised her brows and said, "You know, the Harbor has a bigger record shop than we do here in the Cove. I bet they'll have that new Bobby Sherman song you like so much, Sienna."

The child had a passion for all things relating to Bobby Sherman. Annie couldn't imagine what charm the big-haired teen idol had cast over her daughter, but whatever it was, it had a huge hold.

Now, Sienna could barely contain her excitement. Her eyes rounded. Her lips drew into a tiny bow. And, her hands clasped before her chest.

So sweet. But, Annie saw Sienna held her breath.

"Mama?"

"Yes, of course. We can pick up the new single if you want. It's been a while since you got any new music. Maybe we'll pick up a few more yellow inserts for the singles; I know they break, and I want you to be able to play your music on your record player."

Sienna's only request from Santa Claus last year was a portable record player and a carrying case for the single records she loved so much. The case and player were so cherished that during the long trip north they had nestled on the floorboards in the back seat—so Sienna could keep them close.

When a happy bounce from the little girl brought a wash of bile up Annie's throat, she held up a shaky hand. "Soon, but not today, okay? Mommy needs some rest. Today's not the day for record shopping or yoga. Soon, though."

"Yoga?" Clarisse snorted. "I should say not! You're going to take it easy for a few days, missy. No work. No play. Just rest. Now, finish the tea. Eat some toast if you can manage it. Sienna and I have things to do. We'll check on you later."

Clarisse stood, motioning for the little girl to get off the bed. Sienna kissed the uninjured temple, and—a big, Bobby-Sherman-loving grin still plastered on her face—slowly scuttled backward off the bed. She was so slight that the jump from bed to floor barely bounced the mattress, something Annie was profoundly grateful for.

The ambition, for yoga or anything else, that coursed through her veins just a short time ago disappeared as suddenly as it had come upon her. Weariness settled on her shoulders like a heavy cloak, pulling her backward into the deep sleep she'd so recently woken from. Her eyelids had weights tied to them. Her arm, when she reached for the tea cup, wobbled. The cup seemed weighted down with concrete rather than chamomile and bringing it to her lips was a challenge. She managed, but was quick to deposit the cup back on the saucer.

She watched them leave. When the door closed, Annie snuggled down into the covers. Her appetite for toast had never arrived, so she didn't bother to look at the tray again.

Her eyes slipped shut. Her head throbbed but as her breathing slowed and matched the bump's tempo, she relaxed, able to ignore the *thump-thump-thump* in her head.

Slumber claimed her, and she didn't resist. For the first time since the news of Brian's death had arrived, Annie let someone else take the reins. Sienna was in good hands with Clarisse. Time for the caregiver to be cared for…

Chapter 21

"Man, I don't remember the last time I saw a guy so hooked on a babe. Damn, Steve, this is making the rest of us look bad."

Big Al stood in the center of the shop, his bulk squeezed into one narrow aisle. He turned in a circle, scanning the walls with a look of utter disbelief on his face. His tongue made a clicking noise against the back of his teeth, punctuating the shaking of his head. Every new shake generated a click. Each turn, a shake. Finally, Steve couldn't stand it.

"Hey, cut it out. You sound like you're drilling yourself right into the freaking floorboards, man. It's nothing. Just a little paint, that's all."

The fact that he was on a ladder, screwing a new light fixture to the ceiling while the old, rusty fixture lay in a heap below kind of shot his paint-only declaration to shit. But hey, he didn't need a work order—or marriage license—to do a good deed.

"Just a little paint? You're kidding, right?"

"Do I have to explain everything I do to you? Are you suddenly the town busybody?"

Big Al snorted, then laughed. "Nah. That job's already taken. But really, man…you're hot on this lady, aren't you?" He held up a beefy hand. "No, don't answer. This isn't a yes-or-no question. I'd have to be blind not to see how you feel."

He snugged the last screw up against the metal plate in the ceiling. A sharp tug on the chain attaching the fixture to the ceiling. It held, so he pushed his screwdriver into the back pocket of his jeans. He grabbed the light bulb perched on the top platform of the ladder, put it into the fixture, and pointed to the light switch.

"Will you hit that for me?"

Big Al crossed the room and flicked the switch. The bulb lit, so he turned the switch to the off position.

"Thanks."

Steve descended. He closed the ladder and walked to the doorway. Leaning the tool against the wall, he finally met his friend's gaze.

A shrug. "Hot doesn't even begin to describe it, man. I…" He searched for the words to explain. There weren't any. "I don't know. This isn't like anything else I've ever dealt with. She's just…hell, I don't know. When I see her…when I think about her…oh, God…"

Every day his feelings grew more intense. Every night he dreamed about Annie. Every waking minute he was on alert for her presence, scanning the streets and shops in the hope he might catch a glimpse of her.

Every minute he wondered how much she would hate his guts when she learned the truth about him.

"Did you tell her yet?"

One word, but he couldn't say it. He shook his head. "I tried."

"Oh…you gotta tell her. Sooner or later, she's going to find out. Better from you than—well, you already know this. I don't need to spell it out for you. We went over this already, remember? Don't you get it?"

147

"Yeah, I get it. I do—it's just that I figure once she knows, I'm out. Not that I'm 'in' or anything, but if she doesn't hate me I still have a chance. Falling in—well, whatever this is—shouldn't be such a pain in the ass. It just shouldn't."

Big Al chuckled. "It's love, man. Call it what it is. Love—it finally hit home, didn't it? Not just for other guys anymore, is it?"

"Yeah, it hit. Hard. Who knew it could turn an average Joe into a freaking mess?"

The other guy shook his head and smiled. For the first time, a look of pure understanding passed between them. "Who knew? Shit, man—any guy who's fallen for a chick knows. We've all had it happen, believe me. Some chicks, hey, they're easy come, easy go—if you know what I mean. We've all had those kinds, too. But a woman who grabs you in the chest instead of in the pants? Those are the kind to watch out for. They can really kick you in the ass—or lift you to the stars."

"Why do I feel like I'm going to get the crap kicked out of me?"

Big Al slapped him on the shoulder. He kept his hand in place and gave a brotherly squeeze. "It's all the same, man. That love stuff? It ain't for sissies. Come on, I'll buy you a beer. You done here?"

Steve looked around. The place had cleaned up great. He'd finished the painting, fixed a few odds and ends, hung new lights. When he was a kid, and Clarisse and Henry had bustled around taking orders and selling their wares, the shop had looked this way. Returning it to its former glory—as humble a state as that 'glory' was—lifted him up.

"Yeah, I'm done. After that beer I'll get back in

here and sweep up. I want it to be all sparkly and inviting when they finally get her down here."

"I heard she knocked herself out. How's she feeling?"

"Don't know," Steve admitted. He'd wanted to stop over at Clarisse's the night before but he'd worked late and it didn't seem a good idea to disturb them when he'd finished. A woman recovering from a head injury didn't need a sweat-streaked, dusty, and paint-spattered caller.

"You haven't seen her?"

"Not since I took her home after the emergency room visit."

They stepped out onto the busy sidewalk. He turned and locked the door behind them. If there weren't so many tourists, he would have left the place open.

"Getting busy around here." Steve shoved the key into his front pocket. They crossed the street and headed for The Shack. "Groovy if they could get the place open by next weekend when the big rush comes to town. Already crowded but by next weekend, it's gonna be packed."

"Packed. And that's a good thing. Steady bread coming into town, no one's complaining over that. Prices of gas going higher every damn week, it seems."

"Yeah. It's the only thing that keeps me from getting on my bike and driving off into the sunset sometimes, the price of gas. Wouldn't get too damn far if I just take off."

Big Al opened the door to the eatery. Marlboro smoke mixed with the smell of frying onions hit them square in the face. They went inside, sat at two stools at the bar. Immediately two drafts were placed before them.

"Thanks," they said in tandem. Lifting their glasses first in salute to the bartender, Jim, then to each other, before taking their first pulls.

The beer slid down his throat, opening the tightness that was his constant companion these days. Fear, he figured. That had to be the reason he slept like shit and felt like a noose hung from his neck.

Big Al dropped a hand on Steve's shoulder again. "You gotta tell her, man. Putting it off ain't making it any easier."

"I know. But knowing doesn't make it any easier, either."

****

Bar Harbor was much more attractive when Annie wasn't seeing double.

A ramped-up version of Lobster Cove, with more people, cars and a harbor, the town seemed pretty but a bit too busy. Maybe she'd grown accustomed to small-town, sleepy life—she didn't know. All Annie knew was that if given a choice between living in Lobster Cove or Bar Harbor, there was no contest. The Cove won, hands down.

She looked down at Sienna. They were on the big pier, looking out at the sailboats bobbing on the water. Her daughter was captivated by the boats, especially interested in the colorful sails. She'd been offered ice cream twice already, and had waved it off both times.

The lure of the sea must be in her veins.

Clarisse placed a hand on her shoulder. She'd been wonderful, a compassionate nurse who tended without hovering. Annie couldn't have asked for a better caregiver.

"How are you doing, honey? Still feeling up to snuff? If you're not, we can go back to the car, you know." Clarisse's penetrating stare cut through the big round lenses on her sunglasses.

"It's cool. Really, it is. I'm fine. I probably could have gone into the store and finished up. We've got short time if we want to open in a few days."

"That place can wait. It's been waiting all these years. A couple more days won't make a difference." Clarisse took her hand away, bent down to speak to the child standing in front of them at the railing. "Look— do you see the dolphins over there? Just past that sailboat, the one with the sun on its sail? There are two dolphins. Watch the water and you'll see them come up."

Annie loved the way her little girl took the wrinkled hand in hers and gave it an excited squeeze. The bond between the three of them grew stronger daily. She loved everything about their new life.

Even Steve. She couldn't go so far as to say she loved him. Not yet. But, the heat radiating from her heart whenever she saw him—heck, whenever she thought about him—had to mean something.

"There! I see them!" Sienna pointed, and sure enough, a trio of dolphins broke the surface. Leaping high before landing back in the water, the mammals gave a thrilling show. Sienna's wasn't the only voice raised in excitement, nor was hers the only finger pointing out to sea.

"I always loved watching the dolphins." Clarisse bent down and placed a quick kiss on the child's cheek. "Whales, too. Have you ever seen a whale, honey?"

Sienna whirled so quickly—the dolphins nearly forgotten—her pigtails slapped her cheeks. She looked to Annie for confirmation when she said, "Whales? No, I never saw one—did I, Mama?"

"You have not. Neither of us has ever seen a whale."

"We shall have to remedy that," Clarisse said firmly. "The fall is the best time to go on a whale watch. We will make sure to put that on our calendars."

"Groovy!" Sienna clapped her hands, then her eyes grew wide. She whipped back, facing the water again. Whale business taken care of, dolphins were remembered.

"You're too good to us." Annie meant it, too.

"Nonsense. There's no such thing as too good."

She hesitated, then asked the nagging question that wouldn't leave her head no matter how hard she tried to will it away.

"Why hasn't he called? He has your phone number, doesn't he?"

Clarisse didn't pretend not to understand. "He does."

"Why, then? If he doesn't want to call, why hasn't he stopped by—even for just a minute? I just don't get it. I really, really don't…"

With a light touch on Sienna's shoulder and a steady finger straight to sea, Clarisse pointed out a new pair of dolphins.

She didn't take her eyes from the frolicking creatures when she answered. And, she didn't put much emotion in the brief advice.

"Don't try to get it, Annie. He's a man, and they're as foreign to us as we are to those water-loving creatures out there. We'll never understand men, no matter how hard we try. So, all we can do is—"

They hadn't realized little ears were tuned to their words but Sienna interrupted. She didn't bother to turn around, but her words made both women laugh out loud.

"Suck it up, buttercup!"

Chapter 22

Clarisse turned in a full circle, surveying their surroundings with a keen eye. Annie wondered if the old woman was seeing the past, remembering what once was instead of what lay before them. Either way, she should be pleased. The shop glistened, and she couldn't believe even the luster of long-ago might dull the shine around them.

"It's beautiful," Annie said. "It's exactly what we wanted, right down to the periwinkle-blue window trim. So pretty..."

Clarisse faced her with bright eyes. She swallowed hard, keeping what Annie hoped were happy, rather than remorseful, tears at bay.

Her voice was slightly wobbly. "It takes me back..."

When a tear slid down Clarisse's cheek, she crossed the open space and stood beside her. She put an arm around the shoulder of the woman she'd learned to love and respect.

"It's cool...looking back isn't a bad thing, Clarisse."

She rubbed a hand along the soft madras print shirt covering Clarisse's slight frame. They stood like that for a few minutes. Not speaking, just being together in a special place and remembering the past.

Annie's past seemed distant. Maybe even more

distant than Clarisse's was. Naturally thoughts of Brian invaded her mind. Times when they were young. In love. Carefree. Sleeping in a tent under the stars in his parents' backyard. Trying weed for the first time together at an outdoor concert, Creedence playing on stage while they kissed in the grass. Getting married. Finding out the tummy bug bothering her for two weeks wasn't a virus but a baby. Then, the mail that had changed everything. Moved their hopes and dreams, all the plans they'd made for each other and their unborn child, to the back burner.

Hard to believe one letter could change so many lives, but it had. The frantic few weeks before being shipped out had passed in a blur of teary lovemaking and reassurances that it would all be all right.

It hadn't been all right. Damn it all to hell, it hadn't been.

A second letter, delivered by a man in full dress uniform—the one to snuff out all the plans she had for her life. The letter that left her ground beneath the heel of The Man's heavy boot. The letter that made her responsible—solely, completely and forevermore—for another human being.

She still had that letter.

Yeah, Clarisse's memories had to be better than the ones Annie had in her head.

Annie was grateful when Clarisse spoke.

"I try not to look back because there's no sense to it. Of course, now and then I reminisce, but I try to focus on today. Not tomorrow. Not yesterday. Just today. It's enough for this old woman to think about, the day ahead of me."

"One day at a time, right?"

Clarisse met her gaze. Her eyes had cleared, and sparkled with excitement now.

"That's right, honey. One day—sometimes one hour—at a time. Are you okay?"

She didn't have to fib when she said, "I am. It's hard—looking back—but it all feels a bit...I don't know. As time passes, it still hurts, but it's not as sharp as it was in the beginning. I don't feel skewered every time I look back to what we had. What we planned. I hate it that Brian's gone, and I'd sell my soul to have him be standing here with us but..."

Removing her arm from Clarisse's shoulders and walking to the front window, Annie shrugged. The words felt trapped in her throat. Saying them aloud felt traitorous so she didn't. Staring out onto the busy street, where people went about their lives without any of the baggage she carried, didn't help. The unspoken words hung heavy on her heart.

Clarisse moved on noiseless feet. She stood behind Annie, put a soft hand on her back and rubbed gently.

"But you're moving forward. That's okay. It's just what Brian would want. He's gone, and we can't change that. You need to give yourself permission to fall in love again. It's not taking anything away from what you had with my handsome grandson. It's giving something to the woman he loved—and his daughter."

"I know all of that, really, I do, but it's hard."

"No one needs to tell you life isn't easy. You know, you've lived the tough times these past years. But things that come easy often aren't worth much, and the challenges are usually worth fighting for."

Annie smiled. They'd allowed Sienna a bit of freedom, leaving her on the bench outside the shop on her own. She had a pocketful of Tootsie Rolls, the beloved Maggie doll, and her Etch-A-Sketch. Swinging her legs, chewing and sketching, she was the picture of pure childhood contentment.

"You're a wise woman. Maybe someday, if I'm lucky, I'll be wisdom-filled and able to give great advice to that little girly. I hope I have the words you have if and when the time comes that she needs them. Thank you, Clarisse."

They turned from the window. The shelves before them needed to be stocked. If they wanted to open tomorrow, they'd have to work hard today.

"We should get to work, but first I want to ask you a question. That is, if you don't mind. I hate to think I'd be one of those prying old biddies, poking my nose in where it doesn't belong."

After three days of rest, it was great to be back in the thick of things. She was ready to finish up, excited for the big opening.

"You could never be a biddy. Ask away."

"I just want to know when you and Steve are going to quit messing around and set things straight between you. I've known that man his whole life, but even if I didn't, it's not hard to see he loves you. Why, he rushed you to the hospital, didn't he?"

Annie was grateful, but she still wondered why Steve had come into the shop that night at all. He had come with a purpose but had never revealed it. Hard, she guessed, to talk when the woman he wanted to speak with was flat out at his feet.

Ugh. What an embarrassment! She touched her temple with a soft fingertip. Still tender but not painful.

"He did. It was a stand-up thing to do, and I'm glad

he did. I don't even want to think about what might have happened if I'd been alone. It was stupid, what I did. Not eating, working so hard—and it was so hot in here."

"Don't punish yourself. It happened, and Steve was here. That's what's important."

"I still don't know what he wanted to tell me that night. It just seems so weird, that he stopped in at all. You know how he's been cool toward me. Almost aloof. It's like being on a roller coaster, this hot and cold treatment the guy gives me. What's the deal with him, anyway?"

Clarisse sighed.

"Did he give you any idea why he came by that night? Anything at all?"

Annie thought back. He did seem set on saying something before she fainted.

"Not really. But I swear he was going to tell me something. It looked like he was having trouble saying it, whatever it was. Then...*kablammy*. The fall and smack, no time to talk with a big bump on the head."

"No, not the time. But he came to talk with you, so maybe you two just have to find a time to finish that conversation." She paused, staring at the floor for a long minute while she chose her next words. Annie waited until Clarisse looked up. Her eyes were troubled, but she looked into Annie's eyes without blinking. "We all have secrets, honey. Things we don't share. Sometimes, the secret is one that everyone knows but is kind enough not to bring up. And even though those around us realize the situation isn't one we chose or like, they see it for what it is. And, not to confuse things further, often we're the last to realize that what we're ashamed of or troubled by isn't open to negotiation. Or change. Or anything—it just is what it is, a fact of our lives."

"You're saying Steve is ashamed of something? That he's got a secret, something that he can't help?"

Clarisse sighed a second time but shrugged as she did. "I'm not giving anything away here. Yes, he's got a ball and chain dragging him down. Until he faces it, and deals with it, he's going to be pulled low by it. I suspect he was going to come clean the other night. It makes sense."

Annie's heart nearly stopped. She hated to ask, but had to. "Is he married?"

"No, nothing like that. Believe me, if he wanted to be married he could be. He's been the handsome, sought-after guy in this town since he was a quarterback at Lobster Cove High. No one ever caught his eye well enough to reel that freedom-loving fish in. Until now. I believe he may be hooked now, Annie."

She was glad he didn't have a wife somewhere.

"I didn't try to hook him. And I think…well, I might be…"

"It's okay. There's nothing to be ashamed of, honey. It is time—really, it is. Move forward, leave the past in the past. It's okay—it's written all over your face. You're hooked, too."

"I am. But being hooked on a guy who has some dark secret isn't my idea of perfection."

Clarisse went to the counter and opened a cardboard box filled with tie-dyed socks. She began to pile them in attractive rows, propping a price guide against the back of the countertop.

"Perfection is an illusion, Annie. Real life is give

and take, understanding and trust. No smoke and mirrors—just honesty. You and Steve need to come clean with each other before long. It's the last piece of advice I'm going to give on this topic." She looked over her shoulder and winked. "That is, unless you ask for more. Go talk with him, honey. Go on, I'll keep an eye on Sienna."

She didn't have any idea where Steve was, but she did have a couple of ideas where he might be.

Annie headed for the back of the shop. "Going out the back door. If Sienna sees me walking toward the dock, she'll put up a fuss and want to tag along. Thanks. I'll be back soon."

"Take your time."

As she opened the back door to let herself out, she heard Clarisse begin to hum.

The tune was a familiar one, playing constantly on the radio since its release.

Catchy melody. Sad lyrics. A sign of the times.

Then, Clarisse began to sing. She had a lovely voice, even when it lent itself to heartbreak.

"I know, it's been coming for some time. I wanna know, if you've ever seen the rain…"

Chapter 23

Steve couldn't say he was surprised when he glanced up and saw Annie coming toward the dock. She looked good, walking with purpose and showing no ill effects from her accident. He was glad; it had been plaguing him that she might be suffering, but he hadn't had time to stop in for a check.

And, he knew the next time they met he'd have to finish what he'd started. Or what he'd tried to start. Big Al was right. Coming clean was the only way to go. And if Annie couldn't accept it—and him—he'd just have to deal with it. He wasn't sure how he'd do that, but hell, the chips had to fall where they fell. It wouldn't be the first time in his life the shit had hit the fan. He was sure it wouldn't be the last time, either.

First, to enjoy the unpretentious beauty coming closer. With each step, his heart beat a little bit faster. What a gift, this thing called love. Beyond words. Beyond groovy. Beyond anything—and everything.

He wanted to pull her close, bury his face in her hair and inhale the wonder of her. He wanted—oh, God, how he wanted her.

But he smiled, and played it cool.

"You're looking good."

A sea breeze rose at that very minute, whipping her gauzy white skirt a bit higher. The long, tanned expanse of skin exposed by the breeze didn't do much to slow his heartbeat.

The loose-fitting, buttercup-yellow peasant top hung off one shoulder, showing yet again the woman didn't always wear a bra. Her shoulder looked soft and inviting. He wondered how it would feel to put his head down on that shoulder and just breathe. Just be. No outside world, just them.

Her espadrilles matched the skirt. Ten coral-painted toenails peeked out. He realized her toes matched her fingertips…and they all matched her lips.

His gut lurched, a rush of pure desire punching him hard and fast. He barely knew this woman, yet she'd taught him so much about himself already. He didn't know it was possible to feel such desire.

Live and learn, he thought.

"Thanks." Annie stopped just short of where he worked. "You look pretty busy. I hope it's all right for me to interrupt you."

There was always work to do with his boat, so any time he had a spare minute he tried to get something off his maintenance list. Today, polishing the chrome fittings that held some lines in place. He'd removed them from the hull. They spread out on an old canvas on the dock, covered with chrome polish and hopefully becoming shinier as time passed.

"It's cool. And, you're not interrupting." He waved a hand over the fittings. "This stuff needs some time before it gets buffed. Hey, I've got a couple of Cokes in the cooler. Can I interest you in one?"

"Sure, thanks. It's a hot one, isn't it?"

"Oh, it'll get hotter in a week or so. By the fourth of July, it'll be hot enough to cook an egg on this dock."

He motioned for her to board the boat and put his hand out to steady her as she pulled up the hem of her skirt and stepped over the railing. Her touch was butterfly-soft, and she removed her hand before he was ready to give it up.

"Really? That hot?"

Steve stepped aboard, gave her room to sit and went for the cooler.

"Nah, not that hot. But hotter than this—and it does feel sometimes like an egg would fry on those boards."

He uncapped two bottles of Coke and handed one over. She accepted it, raised it in silent salute, and took a drink. Watching her throat move as she swallowed made his mouth dry. He took a long pull, tipping his head back and closing his eyes.

Sometimes that's all a guy could do. Just close his eyes to the temptation turning his blood to volcanic lava.

"I needed the drink. Thanks." Annie set the bottle down in the cup holder beside the bench seat. She twirled the bottle around a few times, looking at the glass rather than at him. When she looked up, he caught her gaze—and the hesitation in her eyes.

She had something heavy on her mind.

Add whatever it was to what he had to discuss and the day was going to heat up way before next week's arrival.

"You okay?"

"I'm fine, thanks. I just want to thank you for what you did the other night. I don't know what would've happened if you hadn't been around."

"No sweat. I'm glad I could help."

She smiled and the sun grew dim by comparison.

"I'm not usually the damsel-in-distress type. Sorry—I don't know what happened."

He waved aside the apology. "Like I said, no big deal. You've heard the song, right?" He sang a line, "He ain't heavy, he's my brother... Hey, that goes for everyone. Not just brothers. And, like I said, I'm just glad I was there to help."

Annie fiddled with the soda bottle for a minute. Then she put her hands on her lap, folded them and looked up at him.

"Me, too. But...that's what I'm wondering, Steve. I'm not saying I'm not grateful you were there but...I've got to know. Why did you stop into the store the other night? I got the feeling there was something you wanted to say before I did my tumble onto the floor."

And this is where the beautiful chick discovers the guy is a loser, he thought.

"You're right. I did stop in hoping to talk with you about something."

He couldn't make her wait. Bad enough she was going to think him a chicken, no reason to give her extra reason to hate him.

"Listen, I don't really know how to say this. I've thought about it over and over, tried to figure out how I was going to tell you, but I've got to admit I'm stumped. I don't want you to hate me, but I know once I tell you the truth your feelings toward me are going to change."

She tilted her head, sending a cascade of pure honey gorgeousness over the bare shoulder. Her hair hung down her arm making his fingers curl into a fist. It was the only way he could resist reaching over and grabbing a handful of that hair. He hadn't forgotten how she felt in his arms. Carrying her to the car and into the hospital hadn't been purely a Boy Scout move. He'd relished the feel of her against his body.

"Sometimes it's just better to spit it out. Say it, Steve. Whatever it is, I can see it's coming between us. Coming between this…this thing that's happening…"

So she felt it, too. He hadn't imagined it—and it wasn't one-sided. The elation at the discovery was tempered by the sadness of losing her before he really had her.

"Okay. I know you're right, but…" He took a deep, steadying breath. Then, he looked her straight in the eyes. She deserved that courtesy. She deserved much, much more, but this was the best he could offer.

"It's like this, Annie. I figure that by now you've noticed I'm the only guy in Lobster Cove who's less than fifty. I'm the youngest dude here. Every other guy—all the guys I grew up with—are off fighting the Vietnamese. Every other guy…you did notice, didn't you?"

She sat for a moment without speaking. He could see the truth dawning on her, see the widening of those gorgeous golden-flecked eyes. The way her lips drew together, forming a tight, thin line, was a huge warning.

She got it. Finally, she got it.

"I didn't. Maybe I'm stupid, but I didn't see it. Not until now."

"Do you want to know why I'm still here while they're over there? Why men like your husband are fighting and dying and I'm sitting here in the sunshine screwing around with a boat?"

He was disgusted with himself. In a minute, the

best thing to walk into his life would be disgusted with him, too.

Steve didn't wait for her to answer. He stood. Ran a hand hard through his hair. Wished he were in Vietnam. It wasn't the first time he'd wished that were the case. It wouldn't be the last time, either.

Shit. What a screwed up life he had. Other guys wanted to be in the States. He wanted to be throwing grenades and ducking through rice paddies.

Steve stopped right in front of Annie. In another lifetime, he might have scooped her up, held her close, and kissed her until neither of them could remember their names.

Instead, he blurted out the confession that made him feel like a freak.

"I'm the candyass the guys over there hate. I'm the jerk who looks fine on the outside, but has some shitty luck—and it matches the bullshit heart murmur I've had since I was a kid. Hell, I'm cleared for everything by the doctors—except serving my country. Strong as a horse, but the ticker has a little sound that keeps me here with the women, children, and old ladies. Shit!"

She opened her mouth, but he held up a hand. He couldn't stand her pity. Or her disdain. Two feet from a war widow, and he had the balls to say he sat on the sidelines while her husband lay in his dress uniform in a military-issue coffin.

"No, don't say anything. Please, don't. I'm sorry, Annie. I know I must make you sick. Me and my goddamn stupid excuse—shit, I'm a poor excuse for a man, and that's the truth." He swallowed hard, wishing he were anywhere else.

"Steve—don't, please—"

"Stop! No pity—hate is better than pity. Don't you see? I make myself sick. I hate this. I hate admitting to you that I'm a useless man. I hate the looks people give me when I walk down the street. I hate the fact that I'm solid and strong—but with a weak heart. Fuck, isn't the heart the most important part of a man? Me? No good heart—that's enough for anyone to know. You should steer clear of me. I'm not a real man. I'll never deserve the respect someone like your Brian or any of the other heroes deserves. Never. I'm bad—right to the heart of me."

Before she could say one single, solitary word, he stepped onto the bench and leapt to the dock. He couldn't take the hurt in her eyes—it cut right to the quick of him, tore into the already-busted heart in his chest.

And the single tear slipping silently down that beautiful cheek tore him in two.

Chapter 24

"Tie-Dyed Heart is a much better name for this place than Montgomery's ever was. It's catchy, and pulls in the crowds. Good thinking, Annie."

Traffic inside the store had been non-stop since their grand opening on Friday. They had been open for business every day since, and their business had been brisk. Bordering on frenzied at times, actually.

By Tuesday morning, Clarisse looked in need of a break. Wearing a vee-neck, tie-dyed t-shirt, the logo heart displayed across her chest, she looked young and hip, but Annie knew Brian's grandmother was tired. It showed around her eyes.

"Thanks, but it was really Sienna's idea, you know. The tie-dyed heart thing? All hers."

The crowd had thinned since lunchtime. Typically there was a lull as tourists returned to motel rooms for naps with children or hit the beach for some late-day fun in the sun. It was a good time to send Clarisse on her way—even if only for a short while.

"Then we should make sure her bank account is padded accordingly." Clarisse straightened the display of socks, adding stock from a box taken from the storeroom. By this weekend, they'd need to make more socks to keep up with the demand. Floppy hats, too. Mothers snatched them up as quickly as she could make them. "After all, she is part of this business, even if she is too young to draw a salary."

Clarisse had insisted they agree on a salary arrangement. It wasn't much, considering neither knew just how well the store would do, but it supplemented the government check she and Sienna received every month. Now that they were staying at Clarisse's house, their bills were less than they were before but they still had expenses. Whenever she could do it without upsetting their hostess, Annie made a trip into the A&P to pick up odds and ends to supplement the pantry. Clarisse wasn't crazy about the idea, but a few cans of Campbell's Chicken Noodle Soup or some Fanta could be called children's fare—and not cause a big disturbance.

Sienna's college fund had existed from the day Annie and Brian saw the obstetrician, old Doctor Martin, the same fellow who delivered Brian, for the first time. They'd gone straight from the waiting room filled with waddling mothers-to-be to the First National Bank and opened a savings account for their unborn child.

Both Annie and Brian agreed that education was the answer to many of life's questions, and wanted their kids to have every opportunity to learn as much as possible. They'd even discussed teaching the baby— once it was born and able to speak—several languages. They'd hoped that someday they could, as a family, take global excursions. Brian had taken his last excursion to Vietnam, but Annie hadn't forgotten their hopes for their child. Sienna was fairly fluent in Spanish. In the fall, coinciding with the start of the school year, Annie planned to teach her to speak French as well.

Brian was gone, but his plans for his daughter were still being honored. So, whatever Clarisse deemed Sienna's share of the business profits would go straight into the bank account the child's father had insisted upon.

"That's great. Thanks. I want doors to open for her when the time comes."

Annie leaned against the wooden counter behind her. She had just pulled out a fresh bundle of tie-dyed bandanas to add to the display. Holding them tight against her chest, she thought about her child's future. Neither she nor Brian had advanced degrees. Hers was a liberal arts bachelor's degree, with a concentration in literature, and his had been a bachelor's degree in chemistry. They'd planned to travel, read, and save the world—in their wildest dreams.

"They'll open, all right. Sienna's sharp as a tack." Clarisse patted the cash register after depositing two fresh rolls of change into the drawer. The machine had been stored in the back room. It was the original used the day the store opened when she was a young bride. Annie watched the process, thinking the register must hold so many more memories than pennies for Clarisse to treasure. "I know that whatever my great-granddaughter wants from life, she'll get. Why, it's a whole new world for women, isn't it?"

Annie lifted an eyebrow. Hearing something and seeing it put into action were two separate things.

"That's what the news would have us believe. But even with everyone burning bras, protesting for equal rights, and sitting in wherever there's space for a sit-in, I don't see much has changed. I don't know, Clarisse— maybe I'm just blind, but it seems like women are still working hard to keep the world running and just not getting recognized for it."

"Back in my day, dear, a young widow would never have the freedom you do, if you don't mind my saying so. Driving a bright red car and experiencing the world the way you've done these past years. My word, but it's incredible—and so strong and feisty of you! Twenty or thirty years ago, a woman in your position would have been shuffled from place to place at the mercy of kind relatives or strangers."

"That's pretty much what's going on here. You're kind enough to take us in and—"

Clarisse cut her off. "That's where you're wrong, Annie. The shoe is on the other foot with our living arrangement." She paused, took a deep breath. "Look around us. I wanted to do this for years—oh, not the tie-dyed part, that's all you and your girl—but I wanted to open the place for business again. I wanted to see it live again. I wanted to live again. I've been dusty and much too quiet these past years. I closed myself off—and my kids saw that. Until you and Sienna breezed into my life, I wasn't really living. I was existing—and that's not the same thing at all."

"But you have the Historical Society. Your rosebushes. Your gardening. All of that—you've been doing great all along. You didn't need us."

Clarisse crossed the space. She stood in front of Annie, folded her arms across her chest and shook her head. White curls bounced, cornflower-blue eyes flashed and her lips lifted into a smile.

"You should know better than anyone that's all fluff. That jibber jabber that fills a day—a week, a lifetime—is meaningless. The relationships we have with the people we love—that's what makes a life well lived. This other stuff? It's good, but unless it's shared it can be as exciting as watching concrete dry. People. That's the treasure in life. You know that. And now that you and Sienna are here—my people, the two of you— I'm living again. Making my dreams come true, even at my old age."

Annie wrapped her arms around Clarisse and gave her a fast hug. "I'm glad we're here. I love it that we're doing this together. And, you're right—it's really the people in our lives who matter. I know that."

Clarisse turned and fussed with a pile of shirts that was already perfectly piled.

"Speaking of people, have you heard anything from Steve?"

She wished she could answer differently, but she said, "Not a word. I went to The Shack last night, when I took that walk after putting Sienna to bed. The place was filled, but no sign of him. And I checked the dock a few times, thinking he might be working on his boat, but it's clear he hasn't been around there, either. No sign at all—almost as if he's fallen right off the face of the earth."

"Or left the Cove for a few days."

That had occurred to Annie. She hadn't heard the Harley's roar lately. And she missed it.

"Do you know where he would go?"

"He's got a cottage up the coast about twenty miles from here. Family place, left to him by his dad when he passed. Painted bright yellow, almost the same color we chose for this place. With green shutters, and a big flower garden out front. The kind of place that's had generations of hands tending it, each putting a bit of themselves into it."

"What part of himself does Steve add to the place? Any idea?"

"Hmm, let's see… Steve's always had a thing for engines. Even as a little boy, he took things apart to see how they worked, then put them back together again. There's a big garage on the property. A VW Bug parked in front; the last time I passed by it was shiny blue with a big white daisy decal on the backside. No telling how it looks now. But that garage is Steve's safe place, his haven. If I had to guess where he's gone to, it would be that cottage—and the garage."

"Kind of like coming home, isn't it?"

"Exactly."

Annie went for the opening, and said, "Listen, talking about home…why don't you run back and rest for a while? This time of day doesn't require both of us to be here. And Sienna is staying at Heather's house through dinnertime. I'm so glad she made a friend here, finally. Kids need that."

"We all need that. And Heather Johnson's family is a good family. I was friends with her mother's mother; we went to school together. Your Sienna has chosen well. Her first friend in town is a nice little girl."

"I'm glad. But hey, how about that rest for you? We don't want to burn ourselves out all at once. Today you rest. Maybe tomorrow or the day after I'll take a turn. What do you say?"

They walked to the open door and peered out at the street. Activity was slow, which was a nice change from the morning and post-dinner busyness.

"Maybe I'll take you up on that piece of advice." They stepped onto the sidewalk, standing in the shade of the green-and-white striped awning Steve had installed for them. It ran the length of the storefront, and gave shade to those peering into the wide glass windows at their displays. "I am a tad tired. I'll admit that—even though I hate to let on that I'm a touch weary."

"We worked through the weekend, and it's been busy, besides. It might calm down some after the new-shop-on-the-block effect wears off. Not that I'm hoping for it. I'm just saying we've worked hard, and it's okay to be tired." Annie worried Clarisse might overextend herself. She acted much younger than her years. "You go on home and—"

Annie's blood ran cold in her veins.

Clarisse followed her gaze. A sharp intake of breath, and a hand to cover her mouth. "Oh, no."

The dark blue sedan drove slowly down the street. The military plates gave it away before the occupants of the vehicle were clearly visible.

Annie had seen a sedan like the one that drove past them. She'd been the one to open the front door and receive the horrible news the two men were sent to deliver. That harmless-looking sedan meant only one thing.

The car parked in front of Lobster Heaven. Soldiers in full dress uniform emerged from each side. They placed their hats on their heads, adjusted them to the correct angle, and nodded to each other. They mounted the steps to the store. One man held the door open, and they disappeared inside.

Before the door closed, Clarisse whispered, "Good Lord in heaven, another of our boys gone before his time. This goddamned war has got to end before we're a country of women and babies!"

Annie's knees had turned rubbery. No reply came to mind. Two women held the fishing supply store under their care. Two women, each with a soldier off to war.

One of them had lost her man. Her future. Her dreams.

She could barely breathe. Clarisse squeezed her arm, forcing Annie to turn toward her.

"Are you okay, honey? I can't imagine how awful this is for you. Are you all right?"

"I'm fine." Annie lied. "Really, I'm fine."

Clarisse accepted her lie. "Okay, then. I'm going over to hold those girls up. If you can't handle the store by yourself...I don't know. Just close up for the night, I guess."

"Don't worry about me." Her eyes filled with tears. Inside the other store, just steps from where they stood, someone's heart was breaking. It was almost more than she could bear. "I'm fine. Help them—they need you now."

Chapter 25

Ronnie Murray wasn't coming home alive. The army men who had delivered the horrible news assured his wife and sister that his remains would return, what was left of him, but it would take a while before that would happen.

Every time Annie looked over at the darkened storefront or the black banner above the sign on the door to Lobster Heaven she wanted to cry. She knew life wasn't fair, but how unfair did it have to be? None of it made sense, none of what they saw as escalating fighting and so-called tension between the armies seemed logical.

Maybe it didn't seem logical or make sense because it wasn't and didn't. Nothing had changed since Brian's death. How much longer would they have to watch the senseless fighting claim lives?

She kept the radio playing in the background. Tuned to a station out of Bar Harbor, playing mostly anti-establishment hippie rock, it filled in the cracks in her mind when there were no customers in the store for her to focus her attention on.

In the week following the grim news, she had barely functioned. The awful nightmares she'd struggled with after Brian's death returned, waking her screaming from already-restless sleep. She'd taken to sleeping on the sun porch, away from Sienna. It was bad enough she was being dragged into the past; no need to tug the child into her horror.

Clarisse spent a lot of time making meals to deliver to Ronnie's family. She didn't wait to be asked to help the women. She stepped in and did what needed to be done. She made tea. Wiped tears. Offered a shoulder to lean on and an ear to listen. She was the mother neither woman had, and Annie knew how invaluable Clarisse's presence in that broken household was so she assured the older woman that her place was with Ronnie's family.

The added work of tending the store herself was beneficial. It cut down on time to think. Time to feel. Time to remember how it had been.

Still, she felt plowed under. The sparkle went out of the beautiful sunny summer days. There was no temptation in the watermelons or ripe peaches on display at the local produce stand. Clarisse didn't bother to stock her stand. She said it wasn't the summer for it and let it lay empty. A large sign said "Closed Indefinitely", discouraging anyone from stopping in.

Annie hadn't seen Steve. Not once. Not even visiting Ronnie's sister and wife after the news hit town. It seemed inconceivable he didn't know what happened. Even the tourists knew. They asked questions about the black banner, crossing their hearts and probably thankful the dead soldier wasn't someone in their circle of friends and family.

Sienna asked about the news. Annie had explained it as she always did, saying men died in war and that the soldier left behind a loving family who now grieved for him. Every time they had this conversation, Sienna seemed to understand more. Annie walked a tight line between what constituted a truthful explanation and one that might make the fact she'd lost her own father to the same shitty war worse for her daughter.

After listening carefully, with wide eyes and impassive expression, her daughter mulled the facts over in her head for a few minutes. Then, she'd come to the point in a way children did so well. "War sucks."

Annie had agreed. War did suck—and loved it that her kid was smart enough to realize something grown men didn't get.

Heather's mother, Evelyn, offered to keep Sienna at her house with her own children during the day while Annie worked. Annie accepted gratefully, confident that Evelyn, who had five children of her own, could care for Sienna and show her a loving, safe environment. It was, after all, summer—and kids were supposed to love summer.

Ronnie's body wouldn't return home immediately, which meant the funeral couldn't be planned or carried out until Uncle Sam did his part. No one could let the young man's passing go unnoticed, so a celebration of Ronnie's life was taking place at The Shack. A week had passed, and the Friday gathering was five hours away. Annie thought for sure she'd see Steve beforehand. The waiting was killing her.

When the customer rush dwindled after lunch, she made a decision. She shut the front door, put the "Closed—please come another time" sign on display and went out the back door. She locked the place behind her, got into the 'Cuda and headed out of town.

How hard could it be to find a yellow cottage with green shutters? If Steve wasn't coming to her, she was going to him. It wasn't the first time she'd done it…hopefully, this time she would have better results than she'd had last time.

****

Creedence Clearwater Revival blasted from the speakers hanging from the corners above his work benches. The garage was tricked out to turn ordinary vehicles into super machines. He had every tool necessary to tear down and rebuild engines. The workbenches were clean enough to eat from. He hated a messy garage more than almost anything.

He leaned over a '68 Mustang. The car had been a shambles when he'd bought it from a guy heading to boot camp. It was one of those high school runaround cars, driven hard and never serviced. The wear was mostly surface deep, an ugly mix of worn parts and grime.

Steve had been working on the car on and off for six months. His plan was to hand the keys back to the guy when he came home—if he came home. The financial investment was minor; labor was his own and would be free. Maybe the guy would throw him the cash he'd paid for the car back. Maybe he wouldn't. It didn't matter. Either way, if the guy made it out of the frigging war alive, he was getting his 'Stang back.

Bad Moon Rising came on the 8-track player. The steady *thump-thump-thump* of the bass matched the thudding in his head. Last night's six-pack of Pabst had numbed his senses enough that he fell asleep but since this morning he'd paid for his stupidity. Too stubborn and annoyed with himself to seek relief in the aspirin bottle, he ignored the pain and concentrated on the engine.

Engines he could fix. The shit in his head and heart

was another story.

Better to stick with engines. They didn't love or hate, didn't live or die. No pain involved—better that way.

Steve grabbed a wrench from the toolbox near his feet. His work boots were splattered with oil, his Levis stained from working on cars and the rag hanging from his back pocket was nearly black. It was too hot to wear a shirt, so he was bare-chested. He tapped the wrench against his thigh, considering the size and mentally comparing it to the bolts on the firewall. Not big enough. Bending at the waist, he reached for another wrench, chose a larger size.

Standing upright made his head pound less than when he bent over, so he didn't waste time in the toolbox. He leaned over the side of the car, stretching beneath the hood. The wrench fit.

If he could get the master brake cylinder off and change the thing, stopping would be less chancey than it was now. He'd taken the car for a spin late last night, which was pretty risky considering he'd already had three cans of beer. He'd stuck to the back roads, thinking he could gauge the feasibility of using the master cylinder as it was instead of changing it out.

Rolling dice in Las Vegas was less of a risk than trying to stop the Mustang had been. He'd skidded, and finally stopped, but it had taken some doing. The cylinder had to go.

A messy job, but no job under the hood of a car was really without its share of grease. He reached in, working the nuts holding the part in place. They were stuck, but some internal swearing and brute force convinced them to give.

He grabbed the brake cylinder and twisted it free. It was filled with brake fluid, and judging by the other fluids in the vehicle, it was probably pretty damn filthy.

"Hey! Steve—hey!"

He jerked up when he heard her voice, pulling the cylinder from the car with more force than intended. Brake fluid shot from the piece, up his arm and across his chest.

"Shit!" He looked down at himself. The mess was bad—blackened arm and streaks of dripping fluid winding through his chest hairs.

Annie stood near the front of the car, frozen in place. Her mouth hung open and the beautiful eyes that haunted his dreams stared out from beneath full fringes of lashes.

God, but she looked incredible. A tiny t-shirt, short enough that her lower abdomen peeked out between the bottom of the shirt and her hip-hugger jeans, was covered with colorful tie-dyed hearts. The store logo stretched across her left breast, pulling his eyes to the spot as fast as a tack to a magnet.

"I'm sorry. I-I…well, I called your name but you didn't answer." She shrugged, pulling the cotton fabric higher on her body and drawing his gaze to her tanned tummy. "I didn't mean to startle you. I…"

Annie turned, waving a hand in the air. Bangle bracelets tinkled against each other, the sound so soft and feminine it made the Creedence still blaring from the speakers seem barbaric.

"I shouldn't have come. I'm sorry, Steve."

She was fast, moving around the car and heading for the open garage door before he could think of anything to say. He dropped the master cylinder into the toolbox—splashing brake fluid across the floor—and followed her outside.

"Hey—Annie, don't go."

She turned. When she did, he saw her lip trembled.

God, but he was an ass. She'd only been in his garage for a minute, and he had already made her cry.

"I shouldn't have come," Annie repeated. She stuffed her hands in her pockets. "It's apparent you don't want to see me. I don't know what I was thinking, invading your space this way. I'm sorry."

The Barracuda was parked at the end of the driveway near the road. Annie headed for the car without saying anything else. He still wasn't sure what he was going to say, but he sure as hell knew he wasn't going to let her leave.

Steve followed. "Hey, you don't have to go—it's not that I don't want to see you—"

He caught up to her. When she ignored him, he grabbed her arm and tugged. Annie stopped walking and turned to face him.

"It's okay. I get it. You really don't want to see me. I've waited but…"

He didn't let her go. Holding her, even just by the forearm, was solid. Real. He felt more grounded than he had all week, just seeing Annie and holding her again.

"I…" He struggled to find the right words. "I don't know what to say. I told you about me—I know it makes a difference. You don't have to be kind. You can be straight with me."

"How can I be anything with you when you keep running from me?"

Her voice was filled with pain—pain he had caused. If self-loathing were an Olympic event, he'd have a drawer filled with gold medals.

"I'm a loser. A bona fide loser, Annie. I thought I made that clear. What could a good, decent, beautiful woman like you see in a guy like me?"

She didn't pull any punches. "You're right, Steve. You are a coward. You're afraid to let anyone close. You're scared that someone might see the real you—the guy with a big heart. The guy who helps everyone out without being asked. The guy who holds down the fort for the whole damn town while everyone else is away. Yeah, you're a coward—but you've made your own cowardly coat. No one has to label you—you've already labeled yourself."

He felt like he'd been kicked in the stomach.

Still, he didn't loosen his hold on her.

They stood that way for several minutes. Neither moved. Neither looked away.

"I'm sorry about Ronnie." Her voice was soft. Sincere. Heartbreaking. "I know he was your best friend. I'm sorry. So very, very sorry..."

The dull ache in his chest ratcheted up. He had no idea how life in Lobster Cove could go on without Ronnie in it. No idea—and he'd put off dealing with the reality of it since the news had come.

"Yeah, thanks. I...wow. I just don't know what to say. It..."

"Hurts," she supplied, her voice a near-whisper.

"Yeah."

Then the thing he'd been trying to avoid happened. Damn it to hell, it happened—right in front of the one woman he'd wanted to hide it from.

Steve's throat closed, the lump forming so fast he couldn't swallow it down. All the tears he'd held back, the ones he'd tried to lose in the countless beer cans he'd emptied since hearing the horrible news, started to flow. They fell fast and hot, burning trails against his skin.

Annie pulled him into her arms, reaching up and tugging his head to hers. As the tears came faster, he let go of her arm and wrapped his arms around her. She pressed against him, so soft and warm he wanted to melt into her. He didn't try to stop the tears. Now that they'd begun it was better to just let them out.

They stood that way until he stopped crying. He wiped his eyes on the back of one hand, drew a deep breath, and straightened.

When he could, he met her gaze. It was no shock that her eyes were wet.

Impulsively, Steve bent and put his lips against hers. If she minded, she hid it, kissing him back without hesitation. The kiss was tender, a soft touch that took him by surprise. He'd dreamed of kissing her, but after the night on the boat, he figured those days were past him.

Annie tasted of spearmint. Sweet and intoxicating, filling his senses with light and lifting some of the heaviness from his heart. He deepened the kiss, pushing his tongue between her open lips and touching the hidden spots in her mouth. Again, she responded, sending him nearly over the edge with desire.

His jeans tightened, his body reacting to the sexy woman in his arms. A fantasy flashed through his mind, one where they lowered themselves to the grass and lost their clothes in a heartbeat. He pictured Annie under him…waiting…wanting…

With a ragged growl, Steve forced himself to stop.

His mouth freed hers as his arms loosened their hold on her. For a second, he'd held heaven in his arms. Now, things were as they should be. He had no business pretending he was man enough for a woman like Annie. No business at all.

"It's not right." He stepped back. Put some distance between them. "You had a hero—and you deserve another. I'm never going to be a hero. You're right—I'm a damn coward—"

"Don't say that! You're—"

He devoured her with his eyes. Her lips were full, pink and swollen from being kissed. Beneath the cotton t-shirt, her nipples pressed hard against the fabric. And her hair, that wild, honey-colored cascade of waves, hung loosely around her shoulders, daring him to reach for her and pull her close.

But he couldn't. Damn it, he just couldn't. Loving someone meant you wanted the best for them—and he wasn't the best man for Annie. She deserved so much more—even if she couldn't see that for herself.

"I'm a loser. Always was. Always will be. I'm not worthy of being Ronnie's pallbearer, or of giving the sermon at his funeral, but I'm going to do that—when and if they return him to Lobster Cove. After that, I'm blowing out of here. So don't get involved with this loser, Annie. I won't be here long."

He turned and walked away. It was the hardest thing he'd ever done, but he forced himself to keep walking—even after he heard her sobbing behind him.

Chapter 26

The Shack was packed. A sign on the front door alerted tourists that the place was closed for business and hosting a private event. Some out-of-towners, friends who'd grown up in the Cove and moved away, came and with the locals, filled the place to capacity.

Annie considered staying home. After all, she wasn't friends with the deceased. And listening to stories about the dead soldier would open old wounds. She'd nearly talked herself out of going, but in the end the desire to see Steve won out. She knew he'd be there. Even if he ignored her, she would be able to see him. It was crazy, but after the memorial she might never see him again. And, never again seeing a man who'd captured her heart hurt—she knew that all too well.

So, she went. If Clarisse noticed her red, puffy eyes or how subdued she was, she kept it to herself.

Sienna was spending the night at Heather's house. The baby was teething, so rather than leave the crying infant with a babysitter from Bar Harbor, the young mother had graciously offered to watch a number of children, including Sienna. At last count she'd had fifteen kids at her place and planned to hold a sleepover to be remembered.

Relieved of the responsibilities of motherhood for a night, Annie stepped up to the bar and ordered a draft.

The beer slid down her throat like a cool breeze over parched desert, so she ordered a second. There were trays of cold cuts and salads at the end of the bar, but she passed those by.

A donation basket had made the rounds, and she'd dropped cash onto the pile. She didn't know if it was going to pay for the memorial or to help Ronnie's family, and she didn't care. The evening had barely started and already her heart was shattered. The details weren't something she could cope with.

Folks from Lobster Cove knew how to honor someone. The crowd was reverent and on the quiet side early on, but as people gathered, laughter began to fill the room. Snippets of shared remembrances, funny stories, and how-about-the-time anecdotes began to circulate.

Annie watched from the sidelines. She sipped her beer—it was her third—and kept her own counsel. It was hard to talk about someone she didn't know. Harder still to talk about all that she did know about being a war widow. So, she stayed silent.

Clarisse walked over and hopped up on the empty barstool beside her. She wore the week's events in her expression, deep circles beneath her eyes and sadness etched into every wrinkle on her face. The lips that were usually pulled up into a smile without effort now looked almost too heavy to turn up into the tiny smile that was offered.

"How are you doing? Are you okay?"

Clarisse probed her with her gaze so deeply Annie turned away. It passed through her mind that Brian's grandmother could probably see into her soul if she chose to do so. There wasn't much she hadn't seen or heard in her lifetime; how could Annie expect to hide her true feelings from someone with so much experience?

She lied. And, she drank, finishing the beer she'd been nursing.

"I'm fine. No worries, Clarisse."

She put the empty glass on a wooden ledge on the wall behind them. She folded her hands on her lap, attempting to look completely at ease. Smoothing her hand over the casual blue gauze skirt she'd worn, with its matching paisley top, she searched the crowd for Steve before turning back to Clarisse.

Still no sign of him.

"Have you seen Ronnie's sister? His wife?"

Clarisse sighed. She took a swallow from the glass in her hand, swirling the liquid around a bit after she'd drunk. Annie knew Clarisse's preference for a neat Tom Collins so she was certain that was what the glass contained.

"This afternoon. They're holding up surprisingly well. It's good they have each other to lean on. When one stumbles, the other pulls her upright. I think it's going to be that way for them for a long time."

"A long, long time. Any idea when he'll be coming home? Have they heard?"

"That's the only real consolation. Someone from the war department phoned this morning. Ronnie and the other members of his division who were killed in the fighting that day are being sent home within the next two weeks. So, they'll have the funeral and then the real healing can begin."

Annie knew that before the healing could start, the grieving had to be dealt with, but she kept her mouth shut.

"That's something, at least. Do they need anything?"

It was a standard question, one she knew the answer to. but it had to be asked regardless. What they needed, she couldn't provide. No one could.

"Nothing, I'm afraid. Just the love and support of those around them. And, time." Clarisse reached over and patted Annie's hand. "You more than anyone knows how important time is to those who've lost a loved one."

"I do."

Her gaze hit the door as it opened, almost as if she'd known he was the next to arrive. There was no way to hear his Harley over the noise in the bar, but she spotted him as soon as he entered.

Steve cleaned up nicely. No more brake fluid that she could see. He wore a blue button-down shirt tucked into pressed jeans. Black cowboy boots matched a black belt, completing his ensemble.

Her heart flipped inside her chest when he looked her way. They stared at each other for a few moments, then he was swallowed by the crowd. As Steve made his way to the bar, he spoke to nearly everyone, shaking hands and hugging many.

"You don't have to stay if you don't want to." Clarisse leaned closer, whispered in Annie's ear. "You don't need to torture yourself, honey. It's time you take care of you, and I'm not sure this is good for you."

Annie swallowed hard. The desire to run wrangled with the need to see Steve—even if they didn't speak, she was closer to him here than anywhere else.

"I'm fine." She reached for her glass as she slid off

the barstool. "Getting another beer. Can I get you anything?"

Clarisse held up her glass. Shook the ice cubes. "Nope, thanks. Still some Collins left in my glass."

Two hours passed in a heartbeat. The crowd was so thick that spotting Steve was a futile effort, so Annie spoke to the few people she knew and tried to forget about him. It was hard, but she managed to have a decent time, learning a lot about the man they gathered to remember. Ronnie became real in the stories told by his friends. She heard him laugh in the laughter of those who loved him. His accomplishments shone in the eyes of those who relayed the dates in his life that could never be forgotten. The man grew in her mind and heart with every story she heard, every joke she shared, and with each tear she watched wiped away.

Love didn't die. Ronnie would always be alive in the hearts and minds of those who loved him. It warmed her heart knowing that, and knowing, too, that her Brian held the same status. It was a comforting thought.

"Here." Jennifer—Annie had forgotten her last name in the crush of introductions—pressed a bottle of Budweiser into her hand. "Your glass is empty. Bud was Ronnie's favorite."

"Thanks." Annie had lost count of the number of beers she'd consumed. It didn't matter. Sienna was safe, and the house was just around the corner, so she wasn't driving. She put the bottle to her lips just as a bell on the bar began to chime.

Everyone turned. Big Al and Steve stood behind the bar, waving their arms to gain everyone's attention. The place quieted.

Big Al spoke first. His words were slightly slurred but his intention was clear.

"We all know why we're here tonight. Ronnie Murray was a stand-up guy. He was born in Lobster Cove. Lived his whole life in Lobster Cove. Married his high school sweetheart here—hey, most of us were at that wedding, weren't we? Ronnie worked here, he was a member of the community, someone we all knew and loved. And, damn it, he was supposed to grow old here, too…"

The only sound was the huge choking noise Big Al made as he covered his eyes and turned away. Tears streamed down many cheeks as no one spoke for a long moment.

Steve brushed a rough hand across his face. Annie saw the agony is his eyes, but to his credit when he spoke his voice was strong.

"Ronnie was my best friend. But that is how he made everyone feel—like they were his best friend. We knew each other since…hell, since we were in diapers, practically."

A few low chuckles broke the silence.

Steve pressed on. He managed a shaky smile, waving his bottle of Budweiser as he spoke.

"Yeah, that's a long time to be friends. So, I guess that while Ronnie was everyone's best friend, me included…it was more between us. We were—hell, we were brothers. We did everything together, the way brothers would. We threw spitballs in sixth grade—and got detention together." Another round of low laughter. "We ran laps around the football field together—in full gear because we couldn't be quiet when Coach McMinn gave us drill instructions. Yeah, we were badasses. We learned to drive motorcycles together. How to buff out fender scratches on Ronnie's dad's Chevy after we kissed a tree coming home half in the bag from some party in Bar Harbor."

Steve paused. He took a long pull from the bottle. It had been full when he began to speak. Now it was half empty.

"Yeah, Ronnie was the guy, wasn't he? The real deal. No bullshit about him, man. You know, when he went off to basic training, I was so damn jealous. It was the first time in our lives that we didn't get to go to the game together. The first damn time…I was so pissed at him before he left, so pissed that he was going and I had to stay."

Steve took another pull from the beer. Then, he looked up, meeting the gazes of those watching him. His eyes found hers, and for a minute Annie thought her heart stopped beating. Then his gaze moved, and she still felt as if she wasn't breathing.

Finally, Steve lifted his bottle, holding it high.

"You know what Ronnie said when I bitched about not being able to go to 'Nam with him? He said, 'Don't sweat it, man. Life ain't about any one game. This one, it's gonna be a shitty deal. I'm just going to do what I have to do so I can come home to the Cove. So don't sweat it…I'll be home soon.'"

Steve paused. She saw him struggle for composure. Agony to watch helplessly.

He looked around the room, then raised his bottle to the ceiling.

"Well, Ronnie's coming home. And we welcome him—so Ronnie this one's for you, man. We love you…and our arms are open wide, waiting on your homecoming from this shitty, shitty game. Welcome home, brother!"

The crowd echoed Steve's welcome to the dead soldier. Bottles clinked and were drained. Steve emptied his, then set it upside down on the bar. Many followed his lead, filling the copper-topped bar with empties.

Annie finished her beer. She didn't upend the bottle before she left. She couldn't.

She didn't think anyone noticed as she slipped out the side door. She was glad no one saw. Explaining that her tears weren't for Ronnie but his best friend was something she didn't want to do.

****

When Annie's eyes opened, they were met with darkness. She lay still in the bed, wondering why she was suddenly awake.

Sirens. Lobster Cove's firehouse was in the center of town. She had seen the red brick building but had never heard its sirens.

She sat straight up, then jumped out of bed. Too worn out when she'd gotten home, just hours earlier, she'd climbed into bed without bothering to put on pajamas. She grabbed a t-shirt and shorts from the basket of clean clothes near her dresser and ran from the room, pulling the clothes on as she went.

Clarisse, tugging a seersucker robe on over her nightgown, was already on the landing.

"I smell the smoke, so it can't be far," Clarisse said.

"Where, do you think?" Annie zipped her shorts as she took the steps two at a time. She went for the closest window. A red haze hung over the area near the water.

"Thank God—it's not near the kids."

Clarisse stood beside her. "No, I didn't think it was. The smoke is too close for that."

"I'm going to see if I can help."

"Annie, be careful. I'll stay here in case anyone calls. I don't want Sienna to phone home and not find either of us."

She hugged Clarisse before heading out the back door. "Thanks. I'll be back soon."

"Be careful!"

Annie ran through the yard, cut across the neighbor's yard, and made Main Street in record time. As she ran, she prayed the store wasn't burning. Relief made breathing less difficult when she saw it was fine.

But horror hit her in a wave that made her stagger when she saw The Shack. Glass exploded from windows as fire emerged, licking its way across wooden surfaces. Black smoke billowed in the air.

The fire crew was already on the scene. Hoses wound across the pavement from hydrants. Orders shouted from one man to another had a tinge of desperation to them. Just watching the building with the other townspeople who had gathered, Annie's untrained eye saw it was a futile attempt.

The Shack was being consumed. No doubt the last person to attend the memorial had left just a short time ago. What had just been the site of fond memories and shared laughter was now making its way into the local history books.

No one spoke as they watched. There were no words to say, nothing to ease the impact of the angry fire.

Annie heard Steve's Harley. He spat gravel as he stopped beside the biggest fire truck, kicked the stand into place, and leaped off the bike. He ran to the closest fireman, grabbed his arm, and pointed to the building.

Steve still wore the outfit he'd worn to the memorial. That meant he hadn't gone home too long ago. He didn't look as if he'd been sleeping, so either he went somewhere else after Ronnie's gathering or he'd just left The Shack. She would put her money on the second option.

She ran forward, not caring what anyone—Steve included—thought. Grabbing his arm, she asked, "What's wrong?"

Steve met her gaze as the firefighter yelled to his chief.

"We got a man inside!"

"Big Al—he's in there." Steve met her gaze for an instant before he pulled her against him so roughly her feet left the ground. "I'm sorry," he growled into her ear just a heartbeat before he smashed his mouth against hers. The kiss was hard and fast, and left her breathless.

He pulled away and ran toward the building, avoiding the tangle of hoses snaking everywhere and ignoring the men who tried—unsuccessfully—to grab him.

The front door crashed inward as Steve put his shoulder against it, hitting it full force. Flames shot out but he ducked beneath them, entering with his hands outstretched and in a semi-crouching position.

"He's crazy! He's gonna get himself killed!" The firefighter beside her yelled to no one in particular. He trained his hose on the entrance, putting out the flames that obscured the view into the bar.

Men moved forward in a yellow line, their slickers and fire hats glistening beneath the spray from the hoses. The chief yelled commands. He grabbed one firefighter who tried to follow Steve into the inferno, sending the man back to the yellow line.

"No one goes in!" The chief ordered. "Not until we knock it down some!"

Efforts intensified as the minutes crawled by. No sign of Steve. No sign of Big Al.

The far corner of the roof exploded, sending burning tiles flying through the air. Flames shot out the hole. The place looked and smelled the way Annie imagined hell must.

When she thought she couldn't stand one more minute of waiting, one of the firemen hollered, pointing to the building's interior.

"There he is!"

Two men stepped out of line and ran toward the building.

Steve stumbled out the front door carrying Big Al on his back. The firemen grabbed Big Al, carrying the unconscious man between them.

Another firefighter grabbed for Steve, but he waved him off. He bent from the waist, coughing hard. Annie wound her way past the yellow backs of the men fighting the fire and would have gone to Steve if one man hadn't caught her as she passed.

"Stay back—you can't go close to the fire! That building's gonna fall any minute now! Stay back!"

Just then Steve looked up. He straightened and walked over to her.

She fell into his arms, and let him push her through

the line of men just as the walls behind them fell. The crash was deafening. The building squealed like an animal in pain as the fire consumed it.

Annie didn't care what happened to The Shack. She didn't care what happened to anything—the only arms she cared to be in were around her.

Steve was sweat-soaked and sooty. She wrapped her arms around him, pressed her face to his chest, listened to his heart beat and said a prayer of thanks.

Finally, she looked up into his face. Tears streamed down her cheeks but for the first time in a long time, they were tears of joy rather than sadness.

"You're a hero."

"Nah, I'm—" The words were a hoarse croak that brought on a fresh wave of coughing.

Annie waited. When he caught his breath, she shook her head.

"Don't give me that bullshit, Steve. You're a hero—you saved Big Al. You risked your life for another. That's the definition of a hero—in case you didn't know."

He took a deep breath. "I knew he couldn't get out. He passed out, so I put him on a sofa in the back room to sleep it off. I don't know what happened—the place was empty when I left but who knows...probably a cigarette still burning after the lights went off. Something in the trash, maybe...Al always worried about that..."

"It doesn't matter. You're okay. Big Al's okay. Life goes on—what did Ronnie say? Don't sweat the small stuff?" Annie waved her hand at the fire behind him without bothering to take her gaze off the man in front of her. "In the big picture, this is all small stuff.

It's the people in our lives who matter—not the rest of this."

He closed his eyes and hung his head. Took a deep breath. Then, looked up at her. His eyes were bright when he met her gaze.

"Annie, I've been an ass. I'm sorry, for so much I can't even begin to list everything."

She shook her head. "You don't have to list anything. That's not what love is—a scorecard."

A slow grin crossed his face. "Did you hear what you said?"

"I heard," she whispered.

"I love you, Annie. And I'm thinking—after hearing about the scorecard and all—that you might feel the same way toward me."

She listened to her heart.

"I do."

A fireman came up to them and put a hand on Steve's shoulder.

"Listen, man, you've got to get checked out. The ambulance is ready to take you to the hospital so let's—"

Steve shook him off. He bent low, put one arm under Annie's knees and the other behind her shoulders. He lifted her, holding her close against his chest as she wrapped her arms around his neck.

With a grin meant only for her, he answered the man beside them without taking his gaze from hers.

"No can do, man. This beautiful lady just said the two words every man waits to hear, so I've got to find a preacher. Or a justice of the peace. Or someone. But hey, I can't go to the hospital, thanks anyway."

Steve started to walk away.

"What'd she say, man?" The fireman called. "What'd she say?"

Steve kissed her, a fast kiss that promised more to come.

"She said 'I do'—and I'm not going to let her forget it!"

"No chance." Annie laid her cheek against his chest. "No chance at all, my love."

A word about the author...

Sarita Leone loves adventure, whether it be in a distant continent or her own backyard. When she's not off exploring the world, she keeps busy writing, reading, and dancing beneath the stars. Always a fan of happy endings, she's fortunate to have a job which allows for so many of those! She loves to hear from readers. Easiest way to connect? Check out her Facebook page, where all the latest news hits the screen.

www.ingramcontent.com/pod-product-compliance
Lightning Source LLC
Chambersburg PA
CBHW060928180626
46817CB00004B/1444